THE TEA PARTY AFFAIR

Alexander Engel-Hodgkinson

THE TEA PARTY AFFAIR

Copyright © 2018 by Alexander Engel-Hodgkinson

All rights reserved.

ISBN 978-1-989331-07-1

Cover art by Alexander Engel-Hodgkinson

Published by
Dark Brothers Incorporated

PARENTAL ADVISORY

'The Tea Party Affair' contains some strong violence, pervasive language, and strong sexual content, and is intended for mature readers ages 17 and up.

Author's Comment

I have this weird obsession with mixed-genre stories. One-part adventure, one-part sci-fi, etc. Or in this case, one-part action, one-part murder mystery, one-part black comedy. I like mysteries. This is an experiment to see if I can write pulpy mysteries while still maintaining my usual knack for wonton, over-the-top violence. Or comedies, for that matter; since past experiments haven't been that successful. Then again, I actually gave this one some thought, so maybe it'll work better than those disasters—if not in the comedy department, then in the mystery department, at least. I'll go with whatever works.

Chapter Zero: Two Guys, One Cabinet

Sunday, August 4th, 2002—Corbane residence

The office phone rang first thing in the morning. Kaiser Corbane was still sleeping soundly in his bedroom. Alone. Average height, but carved out of wood. Muscles tense even during the most pleasant strolls through the orchards of Sandman Land. Sunlight just now peeking over the horizon. Thin golden rays slicing through the blinds. The still air carried the phone's racket across the house.

The phone went to voicemail: "Mr. Corbane, it's your ever-so-cheerful private eye speaking." A light smoker's cough, then he continued, "Unfortunately, I've got nothing but bad news to spoil this pleasant Sunday morning. I think it's safe to say that your suspicions of your wife were justified..."

Donovan estate—much later in the day

"Have you ever seen 'Two Girls, One Cup'?"

Jim looked up from his notebook, stared at his younger brother through square-rimmed spectacles. Sitting behind his desk, arms resting on either side of the keyboard plugged into his late 1990s computer. Monitor switched off. Modem still droning low. By now, he was used to Al's weird, random questions. Both men were of British descent, evident in their accents. "What?" he asked.

"'Two Girls, One Cup'?" Al repeated, chewing on a handful of peanuts, sitting comfortably in the leather armchair on the other side of Jim's office. "You seen it?"

"I don't even know what that is." Jim squinted. "What the fuck is that?"

"It's an internet sensation," Al said, chuckling.

"Huh," Jim grunted with disinterest, looking back down at his notebook. "Internet, huh?"

"Yeah, you uh..." Al started waving his free hand around, still clutching the bag of roasted peanuts in the other. He was the type to make nonsensical gestures whenever he was explaining something. "You see, it starts off with these two bitches. Looks, okay. Average porn stars, y'know? Piano music playing. The kind of shit you'd hear in a sappy romance movie from the '90s... or the '80s. These bitches, they're kissin', feelin' each other up, kissin'. It's like a run-o'-the-mill-lesbian whore flick. But here's where it gets its fuckin' uniqueness, mate." Al leaned forward in his chair, maintaining a straight face through the whole explanation. "It gets fuckin' weird."

"Mhm," Jim said, not really paying attention.

"They... they take this cup, and they each take turns shittin' in it. Arses like fuckin' ice cream dispensers, mate, droppin' swirly streams o' chocolate ice cream bollocks into this plastic beer cup. It's a party, alright."

Now Jim was looking up, eyebrows scrunched together, mouth hanging open.

"It all goes into this cup. These two bitches shit in this cup."

"They dump their bollocks in the cup?"

"They dump their bollocks in the cup," Al said, nodding his head with a grin. "Yeah."

"And this is an internet sensation? Jim asked, disbelieving. "People actually watch this shit?"

"Internet sensation," Al parroted. "It doesn't end there. Not even close."

"They took turns shitting in a fuckin' cup, what more could they do with it?"

"How 'bout pickin' up the cup...?"

Jim stared at him.

"...and they put it to their lips—"

"Nope. Nope. Nope," Jim said quickly. "I know where this is goin'. Fuck that. Nope."

"C'mon, Jim..."

"No. Fuck that. Fuck it. I ain't hearin' that shit."

"Shit is right," Al said with a snicker. "See, they—"

"Shut the fuck up, you sod."

"They start eatin' the shit, they're gobblin' it up."

"Oh, Christ," Jim groaned, slapping his forehead.

"And then they start kissin' each other. Swappin' spit, swappin' shit. Back an' forth, back an' forth. Like nuns on heroin."

"Goddamn it, Al. I don't wanna hear it..." Jim could feel himself starting to gag.

"And then after they gobble it all up, they puke it down each other's throats. Okay, okay, if I were to be completely honest, an' had to choose, I'd choose the blonde." Al whistled, sighed. "Mate, I'd eat a mile o' her shit just to get back to the ass it came from."

"Christ! Eurgh!" Jim looked up from his notebook. Glared at him. "What the fuck did I just say? I'll take out my gun and fuckin' shoot your bollocks out of your goddamn skull. Where did you learn that phrase from? If mum heard that comin' out of your mouth, she'd lose an entire bar of soap tryin' to clean you out." Jim grimaced in disgust. "Jesus."

"Just takin' the edge off."

"Off what?"

Al shrugged. "The thing." He stabbed his thumb over his shoulder. Pointed out the door, which was open, straight at the filing cabinet across the hall in Jim's full view. The cabinet that had blood dribbling from its drawers. The same cabinet that had a woman's hand hanging out of the top drawer. Red beads rolling off her fingertips and hitting the center of the crimson puddle on the marble floor.

Jim peered through the doorway at the arm sticking out of his filing cabinet, which had recently been emptied of its files, and stuffed with the right arm of Nancy Corbane. "Oh. That thing," Jim said, eyes blazing. He tended to his notebook again. "I told you to put that fucking thing in a bag..."

Chapter One: Who Shot Nancy Corbane?

Earlier...

It was a party of ten. Attending the party, aside from the 'British Brothers'—Al Donovan (Thirty-four) and Jim Donovan (forty-eight)—were their eight friends and occasional partners in crime. Two women, five men.

Jeff Kristal. Twenty-seven. Single. Divorced. Goatee. Top hat. White gloves. With the hat and the suit, he looked like a cartoon character. All he needed was a monocle and a cane.

June Garden. Thirty-five. Single. The kind of woman you'd see in an erotic, yet elegant, painting. Vibrant red dress. Cherry red lipstick. She was always smoking a cigarette.

Jon Whitby. Sixty-two. Single. Fat. White fleece sweater stretched by his bulging stomach. Bald, without the shiny head that most bald guys seem to have.

Brad Mickey. Thirty-four. Single. Thick stubble on his handsome, rugged face. He looked like a bum that had left a business meeting in a puke-orange suit, slept on the sidewalk after chugging five bottles of wine, woke up six hours later on a different curb with no recollection of how he got there, and then walked to this social gathering without freshening up first. What did anyone expect? He's Irish.

'Twister' Chay. Forty-one. Married. No kids. Athletic build. Dark hair. Average-looking features. Not even his wife knew his real first name. Everybody called him 'Twister.' Twister called himself 'Twister.' And that was that.

Candice Evergreen. Twenty-nine. Single. Not quite as elegant as June. Not as pretty, either. She was pretty, but for different reasons. June had the maturity. Candice still looked like she was fresh out of high school—a quality that seemed to appeal to Jeff, who hadn't stopped eyeballing her ever since he realized they were standing in the same room.

Charley Murphy. Fifty-six. Single. His friends often told him he resembled Charles Bronson, but he didn't see it. He had a neatly trimmed beard instead of Bronson's infamous moustache.

Finally, Nancy Corbane. Forty. Was married. Was the trophy wife type. Was alive. Now she was sprawled out on the checkered floor in the middle of the room with her brains oozing out of the shattered opening where the top of her head used to be, courtesy of a .357 bullet fired from a Desert Eagle that someone had shot her with. Whoever shot her hadn't properly disposed of the gun, which was found under a nearby table as if it had been thrown, because a) they didn't have the time to get rid of it properly, since everyone was nearby; or b) they were fucking stupid.

Clutching his wine glass with sweaty, nervous fingers, Charley looked up from Nancy's corpse, eyes shifting from one face to the other, doing a full circle until they reached Candice, who stood beside him, nervously taking a drag off her cigarette. "Well, looks like we found the receiver of that loud noise. So who's the sender?"

"Beats tha fuck outta me," Brad said with a scoff.

Al said, "Sender's the shooter, right?"

"No, shit," Candice said, annoyed.

"Ah heard a bang," Brad said. "Who else heard tha bang?"

"I heard the bang," Jeff said.

"We all heard the bang," Jon said angrily. He was, by far, the most affected by this unexpected turn of events. "That's not the issue here. The issue is that we can't figure out which one of you bastards was close enough to the bang without getting the bullet."

"That sentence dinna make sense," Brad said.

"I'm askin' which of you is the goddamn shooter," Jon spat. "Fucking Irish prick."

Brad stared at him, taken aback by the insult. "Maybe ye shot her."

Jon shook his head. "Why would I shoot her?!"

"Because ye're an asshole."

"Guys, guys," Jim said quickly, eager to add water to the fire before it got out of control. "Simmer down. Let's approach this like rational folk. No reason why we can't be rational."

"Rational?" Brad exclaimed. "We've got a fuckin' dead girl on a fuckin' checker board floor with her fuckin' brains sittin' everywhere else except where they're supposed ta be! Rational! Ah thought this was a tea party! Ah stepped into that fuckin' mystery game, what'd they call it? What'd they call it?" He turned to June. Snapped his fingers in her face. She flinched and shot him with an annoyed glare. "Tha mystery game, what'd they call it?"

"What?" she asked.

"Tha fuckin' mystery game!"

"Step the hell off, boy."

"Tryin' ta figure out tha name o' tha game, ye sour bitch."

"I'm nobody's bitch," June snapped. "And I don't know what you're talking about."

Jim said, "It doesn't matter what game it is you're trying to think of, mate. Wish I could say this social event's gone tickety-boo, but that'd be a blatant lie on my part. Sorry, ladies." He guzzled down his wine and set the glass on a nearby table. "If this were any other woman in the world, I wouldn't be as jittery as I am right now. But that's not the case here." He gestured down at Nancy Corbane's body, as if no one else had noticed it until now. "Instead, we've got the wife of Kaiser Corbane making snow angels in a puddle of her own blood on my ballroom floor. With her brains mixed in with the crumpets on the far table."

Brad sighed. "Fuckin' Kaiser Corbane."

Kaiser Corbane

The man being mentioned was having a stroll through town after having his shoes polished for sixty-two dollars, plus tax. It was a nice country town, with children running around and nice old ladies tending to the gardens that stretched across their front lawns.

Key word: was.

Now he was fiercely pummelling a drunk that had spilled the contents of his bottle on his newly polished shoes. Kaiser Corbane didn't waste a second trying to speak to the man first. It came without warning: the old one-two, a bull thrust, a punch in the spine, a knee to the gut, the bum's head smashing through the window of a car parked on the curb. He wasn't finished. Kaiser proceeded to gouge the man's throat open on the glass sticking up from the window frame, and then repeatedly stomped the poor drunken bastard's face into the sidewalk. Since he got blood on his newly polished shoes, Kaiser Corbane opened the door of the parked car, and slammed it repeatedly on the bum's head until only a pulpy stump remained.

And then he fled the scene, leaving the residents of the peaceful neighbourhood staring at the parked car in shock.

Not only was this volatile man the most dangerous man in all of Cherry Springs... but he was also on his way to the party.

Chapter Two: Not-So-Fond Memories

Even earlier—the beginning of the party

Late morning. 10:34, to be exact. The front doors flew open, revealing a smiling Jim Donovan. Even though he was smiling, he looked irritated. "Ace, you made it to the party after all." After a brief glance over his last guest's shoulders, he asked, "Where's the husband?"

Nancy Corbane responded with a charming smile. "I'm sorry, Mr. Donovan. Kaiser's had a bit of a trying day yesterday and wanted to sleep in a bit longer. But don't worry, he'll be here."

"You're sure?" he asked as he stepped aside and beckoned her in.

"Yes, he couldn't say no to crumpets and biscuits," she said as she entered the large foyer.

Jim took one last look at his lush, green terrace, and the driveway that looped around it, both ends branching out from the road. "Don't forget scones," he said as he closed the door.

"Scones, too, of course," Nancy replied as she headed for the ballroom, looking around the foyer as she did so. "Where's Sandra?"

"Sunday's her day off," he answered.

"Oh. Tell her I said hello."

June Garden stood in the ballroom doorway, leaning against the open frame. She eyed Nancy with disinterest as she took a drag off her cigarette. "Corbane."

"Garden," Nancy replied. "How's the leg?"

June's eyebrow twitched slightly. "Nothing a little surgery couldn't fix. How's the hand coming along?"

"Just fine, thank you."

As Nancy entered the ballroom, Jim approached June and asked, "Somethin' I should know about?"

"If you really want to know, we've been at each other's throats since we pulled a jewellery heist together six months ago," June said bluntly, "she shot me in the thigh, so I broke her hand in three places. With the suitcase weighted down with all the loot, I might add."

"She shot you?"

"She said it was an accident."

"You two ain't gonna start a scrap today, are you?"

June shrugged. "Not unless she tries something."

"Try to restrain yourself, regardless," he said.

June smirked. Blew a cloud of smoke in his face. "For you, baby."

Jim rolled his eyes and went into the ballroom.

Nancy and Jon Whitby exchanged enthusiastic greetings as they took their seats at the table in the middle of the ballroom, across from one another. "How have you been for yourself?" he asked.

"I've been okay. Just okay. You?"

"Could be worse," he said with a shrug. "I missed you, you know."

She beamed. "I missed you too, Jon."

Further up the table sat Brad Mickey, whose tattered, ugly orange suit clashed against his well-designed, highly antiquated surroundings. Amidst the china dishware, gleaming silverware, white silk tablecloth, and shimmering crystal bowls and platters providing storage for the buffet of scones, tea biscuits, muffins, cupcakes, coffee cakes, pies, and rum balls; Brad was the fly in the soup.

When Jim entered the ballroom, Brad raised his hand and went, "HO!" He raised his other arm, which held an unopened wine bottle as if it were a baby. "Hope ye don't mind. Got meself a bit o' wine ta quench me thirst."

Jim squinted with mild irritation. "That's what the tea is for, you sod."

Brad shrugged. "Already got tha wine..."

Al took a seat across from Brad and laughed at the drunk Irishman's antics. "Already got yourself pissed out of your mind, mate?"

"You know it," Brad said. "Fell asleep in a pub an' woke up in a different pub. Shorts are me best friend, man."

Al laughed again.

Jim clapped his hands once to get everyone's attention. Then he announced, "Now that we've got just about everybody here, with just one more on the way, we can begin our socializin' and whatnot. Make yourselves at home. Just don't steal anything or I'll rip your bollocks off."

*

When everyone had gotten what they wanted from the buffet table and had taken their seats, it didn't take long for the conversing to start.

Jim sat at the head of the table, flanked by his brother and Brad. He held up a teacup and a saucer under it. "Now, we've all got ourselves a story to tell. One or two things that stand out from the rest o' those jobs we did over the years. Something so ridiculous that we couldn't fuckin' believe they were actually happenin'."

Brad chimed in: "Ya mean shit that we didn't find so funny then, since they were so inconvenient, but find funny now?"

"Sure."

"I got one."

"Fire away."

Brad leaned forward in his seat. Stood the bottle upright on the table beside his plate, which was loaded with desserts. "Al was there, weren't you, Al?"

Al nodded, having already predicted which story Brad was about to tell. "Right. I was."

Brad hiccupped. Then he began. "Alright, so..."

Three guys had just robbed a bank

In balaclavas and heavy jackets, the trio stormed out of the bank with duffel bags slung over their shoulders and pistols in their hands. Only problem was the old lady that followed them onto the sidewalk.

Screaming, "You thieving manwhores!" the otherwise sweet old lady had started tugging on Brad's duffel bag with a hidden strength that surprised him. "Gimme back my money, you pricks!"

"Jaysus!" Brad yelled as he jerked on the bag in an attempt to wrest it free from her grip. But her wrinkly little fingers were like steel. "Let go!"

The other two men stopped at the curb and whirled around. "Hurry up," Al said.

Upon hearing the police sirens in the distance, the third man got jittery. "C'mon, the fuckin' cops are coming!"

The old lady shouted, "Filthy thieving cunts!" and continued to pull back on her end of the bag.

Brad did all he could to keep the bag from slipping through his fingers. "Sweet bejesus, woman, you're insured! Ye ain't losin' a dime."

"I want my money!" She maintained a firm grip on the duffel bag's handle. Started beating Brad with her purse. "You can't have my money! It's mine!"

The third man yelled, "Just shoot her! We're gonna get caught!"

"Are ye gone in tha head?!" Brad responded in disbelief. "Ah can't shoot her. That'd be like shootin' me grandmum!"

"Well, shoot her anyway," the third man insisted. "We're out of time!"

Brad hesitantly pointed his gun in the old lady's face. "Don't make me, lady."

"Are you gonna shoot me?" the old lady growled. She leaned in close, gnashing her teeth as she snarled, "You're gonna have to pry it out of my cold... dead... hands!"

"It ain't worth dyin' for, ye crazy bitch!" Brad said as he gave the bag another sharp tug.

The old lady came forward with the bag. Delivered a solid kick between his legs. With a groan, Brad went down on his knees. The old lady slammed her purse into his head. Sent him crashing to the sidewalk.

Al brought his gun up. Fired. The shot went wide over the old lady's head. She wasn't the target. The bank security guard behind the display window was. Two shots shattered the guard's ribcage. The guard pivoted through the window in a shower of glass, dead before he even hit the sidewalk.

The old lady shrieked, "I ain't afraid o' no bullets!" Hurled her purse through the air. Al's face caught it. Bull's eye. He sprawled backwards through the glass wall of the bus stop shelter. Tumbled ass over tea kettle onto the edge of the curb.

The third man gawked at the sight in disbelief. "Fuck this shit!" he said. Turned. Raced across the street.

Never made it thanks to the van that came speeding down the road, which flung him high above the street like a ragdoll. The third man did a little spin, shoes flying off, duffel bag spinning away. Then he landed on a parked car. Blew out the windows. Caved in the roof.

All three would-be thieves were down for the count.

*

The party

"Tha jury was comedy fuckin' central," Brad said.

Jim chuckled. Sipped from his teacup. "That'd get me laughin' too if I were the judge."

"Tha motherless driver that ran over Larry got off with a warnin' because of his involvement in tha thwartin' of our robbery." Brad took a swig from his wine bottle.

Al laughed at the memories. "Yeah, I did ten for that. Mostly because of that guard."

Jim laughed with his brother. "I shouldn't be laughin' at Larry's misfortunes, since he's got a major spine fracture an' may never walk again, but... Jesus... talk about shitty luck."

Candice said, "I've got a good one."

June looked at her. "You do?"

"Of course. Why wouldn't I?"

June shrugged. Took a drag. "Thought all you did was shoplift."

"Well, you gotta have some interesting stories from shoplifting attempts gone wrong," Candice said. "Ever have to get out of the middle of a supermarket when you have a full security lockdown in progress because you were caught stealing a box of cookies?"

"No," June said, "but I see your point."

The convenience store robbery—one of many

Candice was running hot down the sidewalk in a sweatshirt and track pants, carrying an entire cash register in her small arms. Somehow, she was able to maintain the wide gap between her and the angry shotgun-toting convenience store owner who pursued her relentlessly for five blocks. Up ahead, the getaway car. Back door flung open. Candice held the register forward as she ducked into the back seat.

Sitting behind the driver was 'Twister' Chay, having been the one who opened the door for her. When she flew inside, the register hit his gun arm. The gun went off in his hand.

Blood spattered across the dashboard and the windshield. The driver crumpled over the hole in his chest. Head hit the wheel. Foot on the gas.

Horn blared continuously as the car lurched across the sidewalk and plowed through the display window of a lingerie shop. Its living passengers screamed in the back seat, bouncing against the ceiling of the car as it blew through racks and shelves with a variety of erotic items. Panties and corsets poured through the windows. A vibrator stabbed through the windshield.

The car burst through the rear wall and vaulted over the employees-only parking lot in a hail of debris, much to the shock and surprise of a cashier who had gone out for a smoke.

Crushed a bicycle in the landing. Flipped on its roof and skidded across the pavement. Hit a stop sign, bending it in the opposite direction.

By the time Candice and Twister had managed to crawl out of the wreckage, they were surrounded by a squad of angry cops.

The party

"I really wasn't expecting that," Candice said.

Charley said casually over his teacup, "I don't think any rational person would." Then he took a sip and reacted to the hot liquid burning his lips. "Agh!"

Twister devoured his tea biscuit and said with his mouth still half full of food, "I think we did more time for the sex shop merchandise than for the actual robbery."

Brad and Al laughed. Jim smirked.

Jon set down his empty teacup and poured himself another serving of green tea, asking the group, "Have you guys ever thought about quitting the business?"

A hush fell over the room as everyone stared at Jon, who seemed to be contemplating something.

"Quitting?" Jim said, scoffing. "The business is what got me this house in the first place."

"Well, yeah, I understand its benefits," Jon said. "I'm just asking. I mean, have any of you, at least once, considered just quitting with what you have and leaving that life behind? Maybe taking a trip to Hawaii or Malibu. Someplace nice. I've only been here a couple months, but to me, this quiet countryside isn't exactly what I'd call the ideal vacation spot. Especially for people who've tasted success."

"I have," Charley said. "I've thought about it plenty of times."

"What stops you, if I may ask?" Jon said.

Charley's eyes shifted from person to person as he finished his tea. When he put the teacup down he said, "I'm not really sure. Maybe it's the feeling of success. You overcome a hurdle and you feel as though you've accomplished something great. It's an addictive feeling."

Murmurs of agreement went around the table.

Jim said, "When you guys retire, we'll probably be the only ones who'd still be doing it. Robbing banks. Holding up shops. Car chases and gunfights. That sort of rubbish that none of us Donovans can get enough of."

"Why's that?" Jon asked.

"It's what we've always done best," Al said, "since 1934, when our great grandfather couldn't find any more honest ways to provide for his family durin' the Great Depression. Turns out he was good at it, so the thievery kinda got handed down from generation to generation."

Jim made a reminiscent chuckle. "You blokes should've seen our older brother in his prime. Mid-eighties to early nineties. Those were his years. He was a fuckin' beast, mates. The crazy bugger ripped Texas a brand spankin' new arsehole."

"Did he now?" June said casually, holding a teacup in her right hand and a cigarette between the fingers of her left. "How interesting."

"See this?" Jim held up a small round ornament in his palm for all to see. It had a comically evil smiley face painted on it and a patch of wild orange hair. "He had one tied to his shotgun all the time. It's a family heirloom. We made copies of these throughout the years. Smoke bombs, grenades, flares—all made to look exactly like this little guy. They're real handy in a jam."

Nancy said, "You've made so many of those, you could start your own company with just those ornaments."

"An' get sued by the Smiley Company?" Jim scoffed. "No thanks."

Jon pointed at Jim and said, "So you wouldn't get out of the business, since it's, uh... family tradition?"

"Right, mate." Jim nodded.

Jon turned to June. "What about you, Miss Garden?"

"Oh, June, please," she said with a contemptuous smirk directed at Nancy. Subtle enough for no one else to notice.

Nancy frowned and sipped her tea.

"June, then," Jon said. "Have you ever thought about retirement?"

"Of course," she said. "There are only so many jewellery

shops I can rob before I get bored. That's if the police don't catch me first."

"What about you, Brad?" Jon asked.

Brad shrugged, eyeing his wine. "Most o' tha time I'm too hammered ta contemplate tha future. But when I'm not, I think about Beverly Hills."

"Beverly Hills? Why?"

Brad shrugged again. "Beats tha fuck outta me, man."

The phone's shrill ringing cut across the ballroom from the kitchen. Jim got up and said, "I'll get that. You guys make yourselves comfortable."

When Jim left, Brad asked Al, "Where's tha bog?"

"Which one?"

"Tha most durable," Brad said. "Feelin' tha runs comin' on."

"Upstairs. Second floor. Fifth door from the staircase on your right."

Brad stared at him. "Which staircase?"

With a sigh, Al got up, rounded the table, and helped Brad out of his chair. "Come on, you sod. I'll bring ya to it."

Brad reached out at the last second and took his wine bottle with him.

As Brad and Al left the ballroom, June stood up and headed for the foyer. "If anyone needs me, I'll be getting a fresh pack of smokes from my car."

Twister and Charley left their seats, taking their plates and teacups with them. "We'll be in the library," Twister said before saying to Charley, "I'm kind of envious of Jim's collection."

"So am I," Charley replied. "I wouldn't mind seeing it again. Maybe this time I can give it a more thorough look. There were some interesting-looking books that I didn't get the chance to look at."

"Why's that?" Charley asked.

"We had a busy schedule that day. Two jobs in a single day. It's really strenuous. Jim can be a slave driver when he wants to be."

As their voices faded down the hall and up the stairs, out of sight, Candice found herself alone with Jon and Nancy. With a knowing snicker, she got up and said, "I'll leave you two lovebirds alone."

Nancy sputtered, "It's not like that, you silly girl!"

Jon was flustered, but he said nothing.

Five minutes later, the gunshot rang through the house and called everyone back into the ballroom...

Chapter Three: Hide the Wife Before the Husband Arrives

The party—everyone discovers Nancy Corbane

"Maybe we should call the cops," Jeff suggested.

"Sure, son," Jon scoffed, "let's, a bunch of wanted criminals, call the cops and tell them that someone in this room killed Nancy Corbane."

"Why not?"

"Kaiser Corbane, that's why," Al said. "Doesn't matter who we run to. Just the fact that we're all in the same room as his wife's corpse, without a solid theory as to who did it, is sure to get us all killed. Doesn't matter if we didn't do it, or if we just stumbled across it, or tripped over it on our way to the shitter. Just that fact that it's here, in this fucking room, with us, automatically puts us on Kaiser Corbane's shit list."

"There's only one sensible thing to do," Jim said, "we need to hide the body." He looked up at the other group members, all of whom were gaping at him in disbelief. "Unless one of you wants to come forward as her murderer."

"Yeah," Candice said, "That would probably make our lives a little easier."

Jim asked her, "Was it you?"

"What the fuck?" she exclaimed. "No!"

Twister spoke up for the first time, "Even if one of us comes forward as the killer—which would certainly seal your fate with Kaiser Corbane—that doesn't help our chances too much. He might still kill every one of us just for our involvement."

Jon looked at Charley. "You've been unusually quiet..."

Jeff pointed at Brad. "I bet it was him. He isn't all too right in the head."

Brad, surprisingly, was too deep in thought to respond.

"Uh-huh," Al said. "Or maybe it was you."

"What?"

"You getting nervous, Jeff?"

"What the hell?"

"You're pretty quick to point fingers, Jeff."

"Yeah," Candice said in agreement. "That wouldn't be too

smart. That'd be about as stupid as... say... leaving your gun at the crime scene?"

Jeff pointed at Candice and snarled, "Or maybe it was you!" His accusing finger shifted to Al. "Or both of you! I bet it was a fucking team effort disguised as a solo mission! You ain't foolin' nobody!" His finger moved to Candice again. "Slut!"

Candice's face distorted with anger. She splashed red wine in Jeff's face. "Fuck you."

"No thanks, bitch," Jeff snapped, dabbing his face dry with a table napkin. "I'd probably get a whore disease from getting fucked by you."

"Drop dead!"

"No you!"

"*CLUE*!" Brad shouted at the top of his lungs. All eyes turned to him as a proud smile appeared on his face. "That's what it was! Clue! It was fuckin' Clue!"

"What're you talking about?" Jon asked.

"Tha fuckin' board game!" Brad said happily, as if he'd won the lottery.

Everyone stared at him for a few moments. Then they dismissed him outright and continued with the general discussion.

Twister said, "You know what, why don't we ask Jon?"

Jon looked slightly worried, though he tried to hide it. "What're you talking about?"

"We all know you were having an affair with the deceased."

"OH!" Al yelled with a laugh.

"Tha fuckin' plot," Brad said, "it thickens!"

"Whoa, now," Jon said nervously, "I didn't kill her."

"Or did you?" Jeff said, eyes narrow with suspicion.

"That's disgusting," Candice said. "You're seventy, and she's, like... forty."

"I'm sixty-two, thank you," Jon snapped. "It was a mistake. We... we were both drunk and... it just happened. ...And then it continued. But I didn't kill her!"

"She tripped an' ye fell on 'er," Brad said with a snicker. "Right?"

"No," Jon said heatedly. "That's not what happened."

"Then how did it happen?" Jim asked, crossing his arms.

"Exactly like I said it did," Jon said. "It just happened."

"We'll need a better explanation than that," Jim pushed.

"Look, I'll explain everything," Jon said wearily, "but I... but I can't do it with her just lying there."

Everyone turned their attention to the corpse on the floor again.

"Oh yeah," Brad muttered, "forgot 'bout that."

Jim ignored Brad's comment and said, "We need to get rid of her. Dispose of her. Figures the goddamn maid is off work today."

"How do you suggest we do that?" Charley asked. "Don't tell me you just happen to be an expert on body disposal?"

Jim and Al exchanged looks. Traded smirks. Then Jim nodded and answered, "Yeah, actually, I am."

After receiving strange looks from everyone except his brother and Nancy, Jim continued, "Brad, go into my tool shed in the backyard. Bring out the saw and the ax. Jon, get the bottles of bleach from the laundry room. Al, garbage bags. The rest of you men, bring out the rubbers, mops, soapy water, whatever. I don't care who, but I want three guys to clean up that table in the far side of this room as quickly and discreetly as possible. Throw out the brains-splattered food, burn the table cloth, clean the platters, forks, knives, spoons, bowls, and plates, and then dispose of them. I want them stacked neatly in a one of my giant Tupperware containers. Luckily I can spare a few. Ladies, sit back and enjoy the show."

"Whoa, whoa," Jeff said quickly. "When the hell did we decide on getting rid of the body by ourselves?"

Brad laughed at the idea. "Usually tha wife is fast enough to get out before tha husband gets home."

"Shut up, Brad," Jeff snarled.

"Eat my Irish shorts."

Jeff ignored him. Turned back to Jim. "Answer my question, Jim."

Jim looked at Jeff impatiently. "Would you rather show Kaiser Corbane his dead wife, and then tell her that someone in this house is responsible, something that would probably end all of our lives sooner rather than later? Or would you rather get rid of all the evidence so that all a pissed-off Kaiser Corbane could really do is suspect us? Take a wild guess as to which scenario helps our chances of surviving." Jeff said nothing, so Jim continued, "I didn't think so. Now get in the basement and bring up one of the fucking Tupperware containers."

"Wait a second," Charley spoke up. "Isn't there any concern

about which one of us killed here? I don't know about you guys, but I'm pretty reluctant to work with any of you after this latest development."

"Let's worry about that later," Jim said. "If Kaiser's coming around, that means time is of the essence. Besides, we're all doing specific parts, so if someone dies at their station, it'll be a lot easier to pinpoint which one of you is the killer. Good point?"

Charley shrugged. "Good point, I suppose."

"Good," Jim said. "Let's get to work."

Candice and June weren't about to complain as the men got to work. When everyone returned to the ballroom with their assigned equipment, and had gathered around the body again, Twister asked, "So what the hell do we do first?"

"First," Jim said as he slipped into a yellow raincoat and snapped rubber gloves over his hands, "we cut up the body into little pieces to make for easy disposing." He looked up at the group members. Yanked a surgical mask and goggles over his face. "Any volunteers?"

No one answered.

"I didn't think so. Brad." He cocked his head toward Brad, reached both hands forward. Brad tossed him the saw and the ax, both of which he caught by the handles. "Thank you kindly, mate. While I'm doing this, start cleaning up that table. Get rid o' the food. Clean the dishes, then stack 'em in that Tupperware container."

The women turned away as Jim disassembled Nancy Corbane's body, hacking off her arms, legs, head, and torso with the ax, carefully avoiding any damage to the floor, then separating them into smaller pieces with the saw. He had Twister and Al wrap the parts in garbage bags. Once they were done, Jim said, "Put those lady parts in the meat locker. Preferably away from my future dinners. The farthest end of the freezer should be clear. If not, then make room. At least then the body parts'll be in the coldest part of the freezer."

As the two men went to work, Jim cocked his head toward Brad and Charley, both of whom had three bottles of bleach and two mops and buckets full of soap water ready. "You two. Mop this mess up."

"Mop what up?" Brad asked.

Jim pointed at the star-shaped sea of blood in the middle of his ballroom floor, then moved his finger all around the room. "I want this entire floor sparkly fuckin' clean in one hour. Don't just clean the one spot that had all the blood. If somebody came around and saw only one spot had been cleaned, there would be questions asked. And we don't want questions asked. Now get to work!"

Brad and Charley started splashing bleach all over the floor. "Shit," Brad muttered.

As they went to work, Jim turned to the guys working on disposing of the evidence at the table. Jon and Jeff were dumping the brain-splattered food in tagged garbage bags, and cleaning the dishes in the sink. Twister and Al were now wrapping up the reddened tablecloth (which used to be white) and stuffing it into a garbage bag. Then they scrubbed the bare table down with bleached cloths.

Everything was going well. Jim had observed everything. He had taken the Desert Eagle and the single shell casing that had been ejected from the chamber, and tucked them away in a Ziploc bag to be disposed of later.

Chapter Four: Unhappy Customer

Four hours later...

Jim figured the body parts would at least be stiff by now. With the exception of Nancy's right arm, of course, which his brother stuffed into the top drawer of his filing cabinet.

"I told you to put that fucking thing in a bag," Jim growled, angered by the fact that he now had blood on his marble floor (despite it being easy to clean), and would have to replace his filing cabinet. "Jesus Christ. Tell me you at least put my papers in a different spot before you shoved Nancy fucking Corbane's severed arm in my filing cabinet!"

"Of course I did," Al said coolly. "No worries?"

"No worries? No worries?!" Jim roared, slamming his fists down on his desk. "You stupid fucking bollocks-sucking, cock-munching wanker! I said, 'put the fucking arm in a garbage bag, then put the fucking arm wrapped in the fucking garbage bag, in the fucking meat locker! Did you do that?! NO! No, you didn't! You stuffed her hand in my goddamn filing cabinet! With no bag, I see. You couldn't even be bothered to do that, huh?"

Alarmed by his brother's strong words, Al sat up straight in his chair and said, "Easy."

"Fuck easy," Jim shot back. "You put that arm in that drawer good an' proper, then drag it out of this house and into the back o' the van. And if you leave a single mark on my floor in the process..." Jim bent down and sharply jerked the top drawer of his desk open. "...I'll fucking kill you."

Al scrambled out of his chair, ran out the door, only to stop and turn around. "Wait, the arm or the filing cabinet?"

"What?"

"You told me to drag it out of the house. You didn't say which it it was. Was it... was it the arm or the whole goddamn filing cabinet?"

Jim glared at him, eyes burning. "The whole. Fucking. Filing cabinet!"

"How am I supposed to get that thing outta here without marking the floors?"

Jim retrieved a Colt M1911 pistol from the drawer, slapped a magazine home with a threatening snarl. He pulled the slide. "You better figure it out." To be on the safe side, Jim lifted a second M1911 out of the same drawer, loaded it, and chambered a round. Then he stuffed both guns down the back of his trousers and filled his pockets with spare mags.

Al watched him do this with unease, still standing in the doorway. "You gonna shoot me...?"

"Not yet," Jim said as he rounded the desk and headed for the door.

Al quickly turned to Nancy's arm and struggled with it. He tried to shove the arm all the way into the drawer so that it could close, but the arm's length was too long to allow the arm to go any further.

"Give me that!" Having had enough of his brother's stupidity, Jim snatched Nancy Corbane's arm and slapped Al around with it. "Fucking idiot." Once he was satisfied, and his brother was cowering, Jim stomped down the corridor, ballroom-bound. "That cabinet better in the van by the time Jon an' I get back."

"Where're you goin'?"

"Burying the body."

"What? You're gonna leave me here when the murderer's hiding in the group?"

"Oh, don't start jabbering' on with your pussy talk. You know where the guns are if one of those wankers tries something."

And, with that, Jim carried Nancy's limb under his arm like a baguette.

Jim finally gave Candice and June a job—he assigned them with the task of loading the Tupperware container and the garbage bags into the back of Jim's van. Once the girls' job was done, Jim told the rest of the group, "Wait here. Right now, we should all stay in one spot."

"Then why tha hell are ye leavin'?" Brad asked.

"We can't keep the body here," Jim said. "I've got Jon with me in case there's trouble. We shouldn't be back for a few hours."

Candice said, "And we can't all go because...?"

"It's still fairly early in the morning on a Sunday, during the summer. People like to sleep in on lazy days like this. But that won't stop my nosy neighbours from noticin' an entourage of vehicles leaving my property single-file. That'd raise some questions, and questions are the last things we want to get right now. It'd be better if one vehicle came and went.

"On top of that, there's a murderer among us, and I dunno about you blokes, but I'm not the type who's content with leaving questions unanswered. Makes sense?"

Candice nodded, reluctant to go along with the plan, but satisfied with the answer.

"We're gonna bury the body parts in a special hidden spot," Jim continued, "I've still got a few bags o' lime left over from the times when I used to do landscaping. That'll throw off the dogs, at least, just in case the coppers go snoopin' around for the severed body parts of people who've mysteriously disappeared recently. Lime fucks with their noses. Throws 'em off. In that regard, we should be in the clear."

Jon had gotten himself into the van while Jim was talking. He was anxious to get this job over with, deal with Kaiser Corbane, and then get the hell out. Not just out of town. Out of the country. He impatiently honked the horn and gestured for Jim to hurry.

Jim was done talking anyway. Mostly. As he went to the driver side of the van, he said to the group gathered in the doorway, "Any developments regarding the identity of our killer would be great. Nobody leaves this place, or else I'll have Al there hunt you all down like mutts."

Kaiser Corbane

The man's day had not been going well. The bum who spilled wine on his newly polished shoes had worsened his already bad morning. Before the phone call to her, before the voice message from the P.I. he'd hired, things were pleasant. But afterwards, things had taken a turn for the worse and had tumbled nonstop down a steep hill.

He took his car out of the shop. Engine problems. Only made it as far as the bridge that stretched over the creak, only two kilometres away from the shop. Kaiser Corbane could have walked the rest of the journey. After all, the Donovan residence was twenty kilometres out of town. Kaiser could easily make the distance in a few hours.

But today, things were different. Kaiser's rage treated even the mildest of problems as if it were a personal attack against him.

In that regard, each 'attack' succeeded. And then some.

Kaiser walked along the side of the road. Back into town. Through the plaza. Past the post office. Past the gas station and across the lot to the auto repair shop that operated on the other side.

"My car's already broken down up the road, you fucking useless bastards," he growled once he'd entered the garage, fierce enough to strike fear into the hearts of the five mechanics that were present. Menacing enough to actually make one of them, who had extensive knowledge of Kaiser's past exploits, piss his pants.

Kaiser was fast. He killed two of them with a wrench almost instantly. Smashed another mechanic's head through a computer monitor screen. Crushed another under the car that they were fixing the brakes for. The last one managed to escape from the auto repair shop, darted across the lot toward the gas station, and stumbled into the empty forecourt under the shelter. He bolted between the gas pumps. A surplus store across the street. He thought he actually had a chance.

A wrench came flying across the lot like a spear, nailed itself between the mechanic's shoulder blades. Dropped him to the ground. The mechanic screamed, unable to move, but it didn't take long for Kaiser Corbane to emerge from between the pumps and drag him back into the forecourt. Once he had the screaming mechanic at his mercy, Kaiser unhooked one of the nozzles and plunged it down the mechanic's throat. Filled the poor bastard's lungs with gasoline, let him choke and spew fuel, and shake about in vain. Lit a match. Dropped it on the mechanic's overalls. Left the scene, nozzle still lodged in the dying mechanic's throat. Gasoline bubbling out the corners of his mouth.

Kaiser Corbane casually walked away as the forecourt went up in flames. He never looked back, not once, as he opened the door to an old Ford using the keys he'd taken off the rack beside the garage entrance. When he got inside, a behemoth fireball launched the forecourt sky high. A thunderous cacophony ripped through the once peaceful town and shook it to its foundations. Auto shop windows blew inward. The shockwave toppled a nearby refueling tanker parked beside the forecourt. Gas prices came crashing down. The gas station followed the forecourt's example; came apart like wet cardboard as a twisting squall of flames scattered it in all directions. The tanker was next, bursting like a stick of dynamite in a bonfire. Erupted. Blowing upward, the flaming tanker traced a slow, lazy arc in the air. Then it smashed down into the empty lot. Fire and smoke rolled into the sky.

The entire property had become a black mushroom cloud of death, but by then Kaiser Corbane was already making up for lost time.

Chapter Five: Death in the Crops

Jim and Jon

Out in a field. Two spades. Lime. The sun was rising to high noon. Jim and Jon were slaving away in the middle of a corn field, standing on a narrow path flanked by thousands of corn stalks that stood squarely in formation. Land belonged to an abandoned farm, despite the healthy crops.

Having been digging the grave for half an hour under the sun, Jon decided it was time to take a break. The sixty-two-year-old man was soaked in perspiration, clothes clinging to his body. He opened the passenger side door of Jim's van and took a seat. "Just gimme a minute."

Jim stopped digging. Looked at the grave they'd bored into the soft earth, which he was standing in. It was only three feet deep, although its floor slanted significantly upward on Jon's side. Jim scaled the incline and hopped out of the grave, leaning the spade against his shoulder. "You oughtta put a li'l more elbow grease into your diggin', you old codger."

"Bite me," Jon said, breathing heavy. "I'm sixty-two. Ain't as young as I once was."

"Yeah, yeah." Jim had heard this one before. It was Jon's favourite excuse.

"All that youthful energy went by with the years."

"Sixty-two. My grandfather was still carryin' logs back and forth in a lumber camp all day long at eighty. Stubborn old bastard never broke stride till his dyin' day."

"Did he die of over-exertion?"

"Nah," Jim said as he plunged the spade into the soil and left it standing upright, "my grandfather was a tough old man. Did logging for a livin' because he wanted to. The amount of times he'd gotten shot in his lifetime—by gooks or idiot hunters that stepped onto his land durin' the season—didn't stop him. Took twenty-four bullets through the years. Escaped a Vietnamese POW camp with a stick and rescued twelve other men that night, includin' my father Jason an' my oldest brother Matt.

"He got back to camp. Ate dinner. Went back into action the

following week and added another hundred an' ten gooks to his kill count by war's end."

Jon stared at him. "Jesus. That can't be true."

Jim turned on his heel to face the old man. "It is true. An' when he got back from 'Nam, he went on to lumber jackin' for ten more years. And killed all three of the hunters that thought he was a deer during said span of time."

"And they let him get away with that?"

"With what?"

"Killing those hunters?"

Jim scoffed. "How the fuck do you think I learned so much about corpse disposal? The coppers never found the bodies."

"Ooohh," Jon said, eyebrows raised.

"After that, he still had another ten years to go before he expired—God bless his soul—and in that time he managed to experiment with every drug known to exist—and overdosed with all of 'em at the same time. And lived. Then he took on the mob when he beat one of the boss's sons with the butt of his rifle—and won after two hard years. Got hit by a truck in '95, then beat the trucker to a pulp while balancing himself on the one leg that wasn't broken. Got severe food poisoning during his vacation in France. Swam twenty miles to shore after his homeward-bound plane took a nose dive in the ocean. Defended a street side whore against five blokes with knives. Took 'em all down with nothin' but an empty beer can. I saw that one, the beer can one. I never thought anyone could get gutted by a piece of tin like that. Almost bled to death on the sidewalk. Then four years ago, while he was barbequing sausages on a fine summer afternoon... this same month, I believe... he died right there on his front porch. In my eyes, he was the coolest grandfather ever."

"If he was that unstoppable, what the hell finally killed him?"

"He tripped over his Chihuahua."

Jon stared at him, squinting. "You're telling me... that after all that shit your grandfather survived... a fucking lap dog killed him?"

"Yeah, when he fell, he knocked over the barbeque and dislodged the propane tank. His cigarette ignited the fumes that leaked out. Barbeque blew up. He blew up. The porch blew up. The truck blew up. The fucking house blew up. And..."

"The dog blew up?"

"No, the dog lived."

"...Oh."

"What was the point I was trying to make again?"

Jon shrugged. "Uh... you were comparing me to your grandfather, I guess...?"

"Ah! Right." Jim snapped his fingers. "My grandfather did all that and more. Didn't drop dead till he was ninety-six, and that was an accident. I bet you that if he could, he would've survived that explosion and lived to lumberjack for another twelve years. If he could achieve all that, you could dig this fucking hole." He pointed at the grave. "That's the laziest fucking hole I've ever seen."

"Cut me some slack. I'm—" Jon didn't catch himself fast enough.

"Yeah, yeah, yeah. You're sixty-two and not as young as you once were."

Jon sighed.

Jim looked at him. Leaned on the handle of his upright spade. "Ask you a question?"

"What?"

"What possessed you to fuck the wife of Kaiser Corbane?" Jim lit himself a cigarette.

"I didn't even know who he was until a few days ago. I've only lived in this time for a few months."

"More than enough time to do a couple small-time jobs with me," Jim said. "But yet, you didn't know who Kaiser Corbane was. You know how serious this is? You fucked the sexiest trophy wife in the entire county... even though she belonged to the most volatile man on this side of the state. One would have to be stupid or ignorant to do somethin' like that." He paused to take a drag from his cigarette. Blew smoke. Added, "Or both."

"I knew her husband was a scumbag. The way she carried herself... the way she talked... I thought she needed somebody, you know?"

Jim cocked his head to the side, staring at the corn stalks as he listened.

"Maybe I just have a weakness for that type of woman," Jon said. "I honestly thought I'd be doing some good for her, just by being there."

"Uh-huh," Jim muttered. "Enough talk. You've sat around long enough. Get back in the grave, old man."

Jon groaned as he lifted himself to his feet. "Goddamn it... you're a slave driver."

"Stop whining."

They finished digging up the new grave about an hour later. Jim checked his watch. It was approaching two in the afternoon. He glanced down at the bagged-up body parts of Nancy Corbane piled at the bottom. She only took up a foot of space, nestled six feet in the ground. "Still in good time. I'll have to ditch the container elsewhere, though."

"Why?"

"Not enough room."

Jon stood at the foot of the grave as Jim casually strolled behind him. Leaned forward as he looked into it. "Not enough room? How the hell do you figure? Hell, I forgot about the dishes in that container. I was just about to ask, 'Don't you think this grave was unnecessarily deep?'"

"And I would've said, 'not really.'" And, with that, Jim pulled up one of his .45s and popped a round into the back of Jon's skull.

The old man suddenly jerked. Face blown in half, spattering the corn stalks. Pitched forward into the grave. Landed awkwardly on Nancy Corbane. He didn't feel a thing. Never saw it coming.

Jim heaved a deep sigh, shook his hands to take the edge off. Every time he killed someone, he would feel a little jittery. Rightfully so. Jim wasn't the type to kill people without good reason, and only then, it was when he felt he had no other choice. The jittery feeling, a tingle up his spine; it showed him he still felt something, and it disproved those people who would call him a sociopathic nutcase. That was how Jim Donovan saw it, anyway.

"No other way," Jim said. "Sorry."

Another twenty minutes later, Jim had refilled the grave with the soil they'd dug up and a foot of lime. Patted it flat with the spade. Then he drove out of the field like a mouse scurrying back into its hole.

The Donovan estate

Everyone had gathered in the study, nervously looking at each other, maintaining their suspicion. Everyone was a suspect, and each member of the group knew that one of them was the murderer. Only God knew who they'd kill next, if that was what they wanted.

"We should leave," Jeff said.

"Nobody's going anywhere," Al said.

"Why the fuck not? You gonna stop me?"

Twister said, "Nobody's leaving this property until we find out which one of us killed Nancy Corbane. In the meantime, we can sit and observe. Or if you'd like, we can just kill each other right now. Then nobody survives and nobody is directly blamed for killing her."

"That's fucking bullshit," Jeff yelled. "What the fuck makes you think I'd go with either of those options? In fact, who the fuck died and appointed you the title of chief?"

"Nobody's chief," Twister said. "Just saying. You walk out that door, don't think we'll cover your ass when Kaiser Corbane shows up."

Jeff stiffened. Kaiser had him by the balls. So did everyone else. And everyone else was unpleasantly caught in the exact same predicament. No one would be getting out of this alive unless they found the murderer responsible and dealt with him or her. Once the murderer was taken care of, everyone could leave.

Brad said, "That's bullshit. Tha wife's gone. Ain't a trace of 'er left. No point in stayin' an' waitin' till he gets here."

"There is a point," Charley said. "It's human nature to totally be yourself when you're alone, or if you're in a frantic life-threatening situation. But in a group, we've all got to maintain a façade that would be considered socially acceptable. If we were to go our separate ways now, we might be off the hook, but—"

"Exactly!" Jeff exclaimed. "Thank you for proving my point."

"But," Charley said sharply, "for all we know, one of us is the sadistic type. The type who gets off on playing with minds and with lives. If that were the case, none of us would be safe, because if that were the case, then the murderer would talk to Kaiser Corbane and tell him that someone in this room killed his wife. Once that happens, Kaiser would track us all down and kill us simply for being involved; and we'd die alone, without knowing who was behind this."

"Interesting point," June said. She seemed rather calm, seated in a red leather armchair with a cigarette propped elegantly in her fingers. "Only two ways out of this, then: smoke out the murderer..." she paused to take a drag from her cigarette. "...or die."

"Correct," Charley said. "Now we just have to root out the

psychopath that did it... and we can all go home."

"Wrong," June said.

Charley looked at her with a raised eyebrow. "Excuse me?"

"I said you're wrong," she answered.

"How so?"

"There's a distinct difference between psychopaths... and sociopaths. A psychopath would have seen this outcome in advance. It's the sociopaths you have to watch out for, in this case. They're impulsive and sloppy. Psychopaths are cold and calculating. They don't feel anything but they're experts in the art of manipulation. You wouldn't know how to find one unless you catch him in the act. We could all be psychopaths and not one would be able to tell. Perhaps I'm sticking too comfortably to the stereotypes when I say this, but I doubt if a psychopath killed Nancy Corbane, he would have been stupid enough to leave the murder weapon out in the open like that."

"How would you know?" Jeff hissed. He hated the know-it-all types, which he perceived June to be.

She looked at him. "I wouldn't leave the gun out there."

Brad said, "Wasn't tha gun under one o' tha tables? Killer hid tha gun. That's a psychopath, right?"

June's sea green eyes flicked in Brad's direction. "Wrong. Strictly speaking, if a psychopath did it, we'd still be looking for the murder weapon."

"And you know this... how?" Twister asked.

June looked at Twister and said, "I dabbled in psychology."

Brad sniggered drunkenly. "So we have a shrink among us."

"I'm not a shrink," June said. She paused to take another drag. Then she added, "It's not intimate enough for me."

Her words made a few of the men uncomfortable. Charley and Twister exchanged glances. Candice shot a dirty look in June's direction. Brad was the only man to voice his thoughts, "That's fuckin' hot."

June shrugged. Rolled her eyes. Took a drag. Not interested in the slightest.

"So we've got no other choice, then," Charley said, "we just have to sit and wait until someone gets tired of sitting and waiting. Either that, or Kaiser Corbane arrives and massacres us once he realizes what's wrong with this picture."

"I've got an idea," Jeff said, "Why don't we brainstorm?

Think up a story that would click together no matter who told him, and rehearse it? We make up our own events explaining why his wife isn't here. If everyone does their part, he'll be completely fooled, and then he'll leave."

Everyone stared at him. The room was silent for a minute.

Then Al said, "That's the dumbest fucking thing I've ever heard."

"Hey!" Jeff said. "It's not stupid at all. It'll get us all outta this."

"Bullshit," Al said. "You're a fucking idiot."

"You're a fucking idiot! I'm right!"

"You're wrong," June said. "All it'd do is buy us some time without preventing the inevitable."

"Buy us some time?" Jeff repeated incredulously. "How?!"

"One: no story in the world can make someone vanish off the face of the earth forever. Sooner or later, Kaiser Corbane would figure out we lied to him. Two: that brings Charley's theory back into play. The real killer could call him up and say, 'hey, Kaiser, all those guys lied to you because your wife is dead and they wanted to leave the house. Guess who killed her?' And three: not all of us have good memories. One Freudian slip and the jig is up." June crushed her cigarette butt on the ash tray on the arm of the chair.

"FUCK!" Jeff shouted.

"Calm down," Twister said. "Nothing good will come out of getting all riled up."

Brad started laughing.

Enraged by the alcoholic's apparent ignorance, Jeff snarled, "What the fuck's so funny? You think this is a joke?"

"Nah," Brad said, chuckling. "Ah just realized somethin', though." He stared at the expectant group like a deer in the headlights. He blinked once, but other than that, he went stiff as a statue.

"...Care to share?" Charley pressed.

Brad snapped out of his stupor as quickly as he fell into it. "What if... those two guys in the van were tha murderers and we're meant to take tha fall?"

The room fell into a state of shock over this new revelation.

June broke the silence, maintaining her casualness. "Now that is interesting..."

"Fuck me," Jeff said. "That's it, isn't it? They got all the evidence. They drove out of here scot-free and left us here with our thumbs up our asses." In a surge of anger, Jeff kicked the side of a nearby bookshelf, which didn't bulge an inch and only hurt his toes. "Goddamn it!"

"No way," Al said quickly, standing up from behind the desk. "My brother's not like that."

"Just because you're his brother doesn't mean shit," Twister said. "Whoever we're dealing with is a professional. We've all known each other for a few months. Some of us have known each other for years, in fact. Hell, your brother could have been wearing a mask since you learned how to count your fingers without screwing up when you reached your second middle finger."

Jeff turned to Al, arms akimbo. Both of them were positioned on either side of the group. Safe enough distance for his next accusation: "Or maybe you're in on it."

Al jumped out of his chair. "What the fuck did you just say to me, mate?"

"You heard me!" Jeff fired back. "You're in on it, aren't you? Sticking around to see where it all goes so that you can give your older brother a nice, hilarious report on the way things turned out!"

Al pushed past Candice, nearly knocking her out of her chair. He lunged across the room, only to be caught and restrained by Charley and Twister. He thrashed out, struggling wildly to break free. He was ready to rip Jeff's head off. "Fuck you! Say that to me again, you fucking blinkered sod!"

A gunshot shattered the air. Everyone dropped to the floor except Brad, who jumped and yelled, "Oh! Snap!" and June, who remained seated in her comfortable chair, having been watching the man who fired the shot since he first entered the room. The bullet went wide. Zipped over everyone's heads by a long shot. Punched into the wall. It wasn't meant to kill or even wound—just steal the spotlight.

Slowly, everyone turned to the entrance of the study, and there stood Jim Donovan with a smoking .45, which was now pointing at the floor.

"All of you, shut the fuck up," Jim barked. "You're gonna scrap, you take it out in the backyard."

Brad said, "Guess that throws my theory out the window, eh?"

"What theory?" Jim asked him.

"Never mind." Brad whistled nonchalantly, looking around as

if he'd just woken up in another strange place with no recollection on how he got there.

Jeff was holding his ear and glaring at Jim. "You blew out my fucking eardrum!"

Jim shrugged. Uncaring. "Oops."

"Think I'm gonna go deaf..."

"You'll live."

"Fucking ringing..."

"If it's ringing, you'll be fine."

"You cocksuckin'..."

Charley asked, "Where's Jon?"

Jim answered, "Where he's always been—in Nancy Corbane's resting place."

"I don't follow...?" Charley said, eyebrows furrowed.

"I shot the bastard and dumped him in the grave with her. Perfect for each other."

Everyone stared at Jim in shock. This time, even June and Brad were surprised.

Jeff asked, "Why the fuck did you shoot him?!"

Al said, "Yeah, that's... that's, uh... not... suspicious at all..."

Charley had been rendered speechless by the news.

Jim looked around the room at all the shocked and confused faces. "What? The guy was a major risk. Sure, Kaiser Corbane's wife might be missing, but Christ. For all we know, Kaiser Corbane knows about their little relationship."

"...And if he didn't?" Charley asked, clearly upset by this.

Jim shrugged. "Can't be too careful. I couldn't take the risk. Keepin' him with us, alive and well, would've been just as deadly. Wasn't gonna risk it. We're risking enough already without his help. I thought, 'fuck that,' and shot him. I made quick work of it. Didn't even feel it. Got 'im in the back o' the noggin. I know, he was an acquaintance of ours—especially yours, Charley, sorry—"

"What?" Charley snapped.

"But... you know, it's him or us. It sure as hell ain't gonna be me."

"So you shot him in the back?" Charley said in disgust.

"Back of the head."

"Same thing!" Jeff snapped.

"No, you can survive a shot in the back, depending on where the bullet hits you. And believe me when I say that that shit hurts.

Bullet to the head..." Jim shrugged, cocked his head to the side. "...not so much."

"You're a fuckin' scumbag," Jeff said. "I bet you're the murderer!"

"Bullshit."

"Uh-huh. 'Bullshit,' my ass!" Jeff exclaimed, pointing an accusatory finger at Jim. "You don't seem too broken up about the fact you just whacked an old man from behind. And could it really be a coincidence that both of the people who died today got their fuckin' heads blown off?"

Jim scoffed. "I'm not sure I like your tone," he quipped.

Al jumped to defend his brother. "Wait a goddamn minute. He doesn't kill unless he feels he had to." He turned to Jim and added, "And you had to, right?"

"The guy fucked Corbane's wife. Bastard might've known about it. Hell, that might be why he's on his way down here in the first place. In which case, we would've done him a favour. And hell, I did you guys a fuckin' favour."

"How?" Charley asked.

"When he gets here, we can just tell 'im the two lovebirds ran off into the sunset an' went into hiding to start a new life. End of story. He goes on searching. We go on with our lives."

"Except," Candice said, "there's the murderer thing."

Jim squinted. Eyed each person in turn. "Yeah, the murderer. Somethin' tells me I missed this part of the conversation."

Twister decided to fill him in as briefly as possible. "We figure if we leave, the murderer could decide to play games and tell Kaiser Corbane that we killed his wife once he's at a safe distance. Kaiser hunts us down and unintentionally ties up all loose ends, and the killer goes free without having to worry about anything."

"Aw, shit," Jim said. "That makes sense. I hate when things make sense."

"And then some," Brad said. "We got ourselves a pickle we might die from either way if we don't play our fuckin' cards right." He took a crystal bottle of bourbon and started sipping it. "Drink up before we ain't got a chance to."

Jim sighed. He hadn't put his gun away since he entered the study. It made everyone else a little nervous. Jim turned to his brother and asked, "What's the status on that cabinet?"

"It's in my van."

"Get it outta here."

"Where to?"

"Anywhere outside of a fifty kilometre radius from here."

"Fuckin' seriously?"

Jim glared at Al. Handed him his .45. "Do it." He turned to the group and said, "Someone go with him."

"Why?" Jeff snapped. "So that you guys can kill someone else off? Fuck that. You even gave him a gun! Where's my gun, huh?"

Jim looked at him. Drew his second .45. Raised his pistol until Jeff could see down the barrel. "You just nominated yourself as the chauffeur, bucko."

Jeff stared at the gun with shock. "You can't be fucking serious!"

"Bloody serious," Jim hissed. He turned to his brother. "You're still here?"

Taking the hint, Al quickly left the study.

Jim looked at Jeff again. "Go on, now. You make sure my brother comes back in one piece. Or I'll find you."

Jim and Jeff had a staring competition. It lasted for ten tense seconds.

Jim broke the intense silence. "Get your arse out of my study."

Jeff broke into a run. He scrambled past Jim and disappeared into the hall.

Jim lowered his gun and turned to the others. Twister and Charley wore no expression on their faces, betraying nothing. Candice was staring at him as if he'd grown a second head. June was smoking another cigarette in her chair. Brad was halfway through the bourbon supply. "Hope that wasn't too alarming."

"Oh, no," June said sarcastically, "you only threatened one of your party guests with a gun while we struggle to figure out which of us is the murderer of a vicious gangster's wife. That's not at all bound to raise a few suspicions."

Frowning, Jim tucked his gun in the back of his pants. "I apologize. Like I said before, you can't be too careful. Suspect me all you want. Soon enough I'll be in the clear."

"You sound sure of yourself," Charley said.

"That's because I'm innocent of all charges."

"Except for Jon's murder," Twister said.

Jim cringed. Said regretfully, "It was necessary. It wasn't out of spite."

"Why should we believe you?" Charley asked.

"Because I did him in quick." Jim turned. Headed out the door.

"Where're you going?" Charley asked.

"Getting myself a sandwich. Free labour makes me hungry."

Charley and Twister exchanged looks.

Brad finished the bourbon and belched.

Chapter Six: Luau of Pain

Kaiser Corbane

He was on the outskirts of town. Doing 50 on the long country road that sliced through crop fields like a needle. The truck was running low on gas. If he'd known that the truck was low on fuel, he would have gassed up, and wouldn't have left such a fiery spectacle behind. He regretted neglecting to check it sooner. There was a gas station just three kilometres up the road. He hoped the truck would take him that far.

He wasn't in the mood to walk.

Pulling into the station forecourt proved strenuous for the truck because it stopped right on the curb. Kaiser had to get out and push the damn thing across the forecourt to the nearest pump. He was relieved that he at least didn't have to push it far. For once today, something happened without proving to be too much of a problem.

He glanced down at his shoe. Under a layer of dirt, he could see the dark wine stain on the toe. "Goddamn bums," he muttered in disgust, roughly jerking the nozzle off the hook and stabbing it into the truck. He squeezed the lever in a whitening fist. Felt the gas shoot through the hose.

He looked up, peered over the cargo bed and saw a colourful-looking bar on the other side of the road. It looked like a log cabin with fake palm trees lining the front, ten feet from each other, bordering the parking lot, hanging lazily over pickup trucks and a lineup of parked motorcycles. Above the fake bamboo-and-thatch entrance was a large green neon sign with a coconut tree outline and 'HARD TICKET TO PARADISE' scribbled fancily in yellow.

Kaiser could use a drink after such a trying early morning. He turned to the gas station attendant, who had been standing by in his greasy faded overalls. "I want a full tank."

"Where're you going?"

Kaiser pointed at the bar as he rounded his pickup, leaving the nozzle lodged in the truck.

"Oh," the attendant said quietly as he tended to the nozzle.

*

On the other side of the double door entrance, loud surfer music assaulted his eardrums while the rich smell of alcohol and battered fish blew in his face like a beach breeze. In the back, a group of bikers dressed in stereotypical biker gang fashion (bandannas, leather vests, scraggly beards, tattoos, etc.), were acting rowdy whilst playing pool, guzzling pints of beer, and harassing the scantily dressed waitresses every chance they got. Kaiser stared at the group for a moment, watching as a tubby biker slapped a passing waitress's ass and laughed at her angry reaction. White T-shirts to emphasize their large breasts, exposed midriffs, and ripped denim jeans seemed to be the bar's dress code for all the women.

With a snort, Kaiser went to the bar and sat on a stool.

The bartender looked at him and asked, "What'll it be?"

"Something wet," Kaiser muttered.

The bartender shrugged off Kaiser's sarcasm. He was used to it by now. Selected a bottle of Labatt's off the shelf. Slid it across the counter into Kaiser's hand. "You want a glass?"

Kaiser twisted the tab off with his teeth and spat it to the side where there were no patrons present. It clacked against the wall beside the front entrance. "No."

"Alright," the bartender said. "Can I get you anythin' else?"

"No," Kaiser said again, taking a swig from his bottle.

One of the bikers positioned his cue stick all wrong as he aimed for the 8 ball. It was obvious he didn't even know how to play pool. Shoved violently. Launched the 8 ball off the table. It whizzed across the bar. Kaiser's beer bottle chinked, splashing his beer everywhere, soaking him. The ball punched through a window and skipped across the parking lot.

Kaiser still held the bottle neck in his three fingers. He stared at it, dead-eyed. Gave nothing away as he turned to identify the one responsible, hard face dripping with beer foam.

The biker laughed heartily as he crossed the bar, nudged Kaiser's shoulder. He looked out the broken window in a vain attempt to spot the 8 ball he'd just fired. "Nope! It's gone!"

His buddies laughed. Shook the building with their thunderous uproar. The biker headed toward the pool table again.

Kaiser grabbed his arm, stopping him dead in his tracks. "You owe me a drink."

The biker turned, and looked Kaiser straight in the eyes with arrogant defiance. "Oh yeah? I don't owe you shit." His putrid breath smelled like beer and cigarettes. Yellow teeth. Beard, an orange tangled mess with bits of food still in it. "Get lost," he said as he jerked his arm out of Kaiser's hand. Turned to go.

Kaiser snatched the back of the bastard's vest. Slammed his face into the countertop. Threatened his left eye with the broken bottle neck. "I said you owe me a drink."

"Hey, man!" the biker protested. Mysteriously, his tough-guy persona had completely vanished. Now he was a snivelling little bitch.

Kaiser's bitch.

"Let go of me, you prick!"

Kaiser casually looked at the bartender, still holding the biker's head down. "Bartender. Another beer." The biker struggled. Kaiser lifted his head up and smacked it against the countertop again. "Put it on his tab."

"Hey!"

Kaiser looked over his shoulder and found himself surrounded by his new friend's biker buddies. All twelve of them. All bigger than him.

"You better let him go," a bald, bearded giant growled, gripping a cue stick like a spear.

"Or what?" Kaiser challenged.

The bald biker chuckled. "Or what? Or I kick your fuckin' ass up an' down this goddamn road."

"Your boyfriend owes me a beer."

"He ain't my boyfriend, and you ain't gettin' shit. I suggest you run home before you get hurt."

Kaiser's patience had reached its limit. "I'm gonna count to five."

"I'm gonna count to three," the bald biker shot back.

"Then I'm going to count to one. If your buddy still refuses to buy me that drink he owes me, I'm going to split your skulls like lumber." Split-second pause, then: "One."

8-Ball Biker flew screaming out the front window. Sailed through the air in a shower of glass. Crashed in the cargo bed of a parked truck. The sheer force of the throw broke his neck and splintered most of the windows in the cab. The windshield crystallized.

Inside, Kaiser drove his heel in a biker's gut and punched his nose into his brain. Propelled him through a table.

Baldie swung his cue stick. Kaiser caught it, snapped the end off. Crushed the biker's Adam's apple with the blunt end. Promptly stabbed the splintery end through another participant's left eye. Sent the fucker reeling, screaming, thrashing; stumbling against the juke box.

Another biker charged him. Kaiser stopped him dead with a raised foot. Both hands on the doubled-over biker's shoulders. Flung him over the counter like a ragdoll.

By then, the waitresses got themselves the hell out of there. The bartender made an annoyed frown and poured himself beer in his own special mug. Took a sip. Ducked as Kaiser's recent victim flew over the counter and crashed into the shelf behind him, spilling booze in a sparkling cascade. "Goddamn it."

A tall biker threw a punch. Quick as lightning, Kaiser caught the fist. Decked the biker before he could come up with a counter. Smashed a table to splinters with his body. Twisted his arm with a sickening snap. Stomped his windpipe closed.

"You motherfucker!" Two bikers descended on him at once. Vicious. Broken bottles raised overhead like maces. Kaiser whirled, planted his heel into the left biker's face. Left biker stumbled while the right biker pounced. Rained jagged bottle shards on Kaiser's head.

Kaiser blocked with a stool. Twirled it. Stool legs caught the biker's arm in a hold. Kaiser's bone-crunching kick shattered the bottle neck in the biker's fist. The biker screamed as Kaiser spun him around as the world's first human mallet. Head went crashing through the front of the counter.

The bartender raised an eyebrow as his shotgun dropped out of the hidden compartment under the counter due to the sudden lack of space.

The left biker came back for seconds, this time with a wicked-looking switchblade. Thrust it for Kaiser's neck. Kaiser blurred. Suddenly appeared behind the left biker. Smashed his elbow inward. Folded the biker's arm abnormally. His own knife pierced his shoulder blade. Still gripping the shrieking biker's broken arm, Kaiser snapped the bastard's wrist as he twisted the knife in deep. Yanked it out. Buried the blade just above its owner's collarbone and carved bologna slices out of his throat.

Yet another lucky winner charged Kaiser without assessing the situation. Paid for it with his life the instant Kaiser's palm plowed his nose into his brain. He fell back, dead, pulling a bunch of 'Employee of the Month' plaques off the wall with him.

Three left.

One of them ripped the fire axe out of the glass case on the wall. Another snapped his cue stick over his knee and raised both ends like splintery batons. The third and final biker emerged from the kitchen with a cleaver, and pushed the bartender out of his way as he stomped behind the counter. All of them surrounded Kaiser. Not that he was scared.

Their desperation amused him. Maybe it was the trying day getting to him, where even the sickest acts of violence brought a smile to his face. Kaiser's sense of humour turned violent on a bad day.

Cleaver. Cue Stick. Fire Axe. Those are their names for the rest of their short existence.

Fire Axe and Cue Stick charged him from two different sides. Cleaver hadn't moved from behind the counter, but he was ready.

Fire Axe swung for a beheading. Kaiser ducked and kicked him in the shin.

Cue Stick reached him; attacked. Kaiser's arms shielded either side of his head from a good bludgeoning. In the meantime, Cue Stick was wide open to receive the toe of Kaiser's boot in his groin. Down he went.

Fire Axe got back up. Swung awkwardly. Kaiser dodged it, stepped back—

Cleaver lurched over the counter and wrapped his arms around Kaiser's throat from behind. Held his knife on Kaiser's throat. "I got 'im!"

Fire Axe sneered triumphantly as he raised his axe overhead for a skull-splitting good time. "Hold him still!"

Axe came down. Kaiser snatched the cleaver, took Cleaver's arm. Let his feet slide out from under him. Fell to the floor. Dragged Cleaver over the counter with him.

Axe dug into Cleaver's back. Cleaver screamed.

Kaiser messily chopped Fire Axe's left foot off at the ankle. Fire Axe howled. Released his weapon, which was still stuck in Cleaver's back, and spun away. Awkwardly hopped on his other foot toward the door. Kaiser hurled the meat cleaver. Watched it sing across the bar like a loosed arrow.

Fire Axe tumbled onto the front steps at the bar's entrance with the cleaver sticking out from between his shoulder blades.

Cue Stick had gotten back up. Kaiser grabbed his batons and slammed his heel in Cue Stick's chest. Cue Stick went flying without his batons. Flipped over a chair. Toppled to the floor like a ragdoll.

Kaiser tossed the batons away, followed Cue Stick casually as the terrified biker crawled over to the juke box as if it would be his saviour.

It didn't save him.

Kaiser lifted him up by the stupid braided ponytail protruding from the back of his head. Smacked his face off the juke box. Elton John played. Cue Stick's face cracked the plastic cover. Johnny Cash took over. Cue Stick's head broke through the plastic cover. Every impact changed the artist. The Jackson Five. Elvis. Shaun Cassidy. Five more artists that Kaiser couldn't be bothered to name.

Kaiser had had enough. Dropped the bastard to the floor with his head resembling a watermelon after it'd been run over by a truck. Left him to bleed with his buddies. Sat on a stool at the counter. "Bartender."

The bartender calmly approached him as if what he'd just seen had never happened. "What'll it be?"

"Another beer. Same brand."

"Gotcha."

"Thanks." Kaiser got his beer. Drank it slowly, glaring at the shelf he'd just thrown one of the bikers through as if he'd chosen it to be his next target.

"You know, son, you really fucked my bar up," the bartender said as he surveyed the aftermath of Kaiser's wrath.

Kaiser turned on his stool. Looked over the trashed bar. Turned back to the bartender. "Put it on their tab."

"I think their tab's just run out."

"Shame," Kaiser said, taking another sip.

The bartender observed him for a few moments. Aged eyes studied the forty-four-year-old ex-enforcer. "You know what you look like?"

"What do I look like?" Kaiser asked, figuring he'd humour the old man.

"You look like a man on a mission."

"Very observant of you."

"It's quiet around these parts, but every once in a while, somebody shows up with a specific goal in mind. An' they'll do anything to reach that goal. Kill anyone. Destroy anything. Survive everything."

Kaiser looked at him over his bottle.

"What's your goal?" the bartender asked.

Kaiser hesitated. Then: "My wife. She's at a tea party."

"A tea party, huh?"

"There's also a man there. Brother of a crackpot. That man fucked my wife."

"The crackpot?"

"The brother."

"Oh."

"Yep." Kaiser nursed his beer.

"So you're going over there to kill the man who fucked your wife?"

"I'm going to kill them all."

"All?"

"The man who fucked my wife. My wife. And her friends."

"Why her friends?"

"They knew and they never told tell me. They let it go on. Makes them just as guilty."

"And if they didn't know?"

"Then they didn't know. Doesn't matter either way."

"That's all?"

"That's all."

"What kind of man slaughters a party full of people who may have only have the slightest involvement in a personal matter?" The bartender got himself a bottle of beer from the cooler. "Just seems like wanton violence, if I do say so myself."

"I don't know," Kaiser said, "maybe it's the same kind who piles up biker corpses in a nice little bar."

The bartender shrugged. "Maybe. It's none of my business, son. Simply throwin' my two cents into the hat."

"I've already got a full dollar in change. Why do you wanna complicate things?"

"Helps build up to another dollar, my friend. It ain't much, but it's a start."

"What're you trying to say, old man?"

The bartender shrugged. "Wouldn't it be better if you could

just... move on? Is she really worth it? Are the rest of them?"

"I'm simply going to trample all over those who make a living trampling on other people. They're all thieves. They've all stolen from someone, broken into someplace here, and further upset the so-called 'quietness' this countryside's got going for it. But... this time, they just happened to trample on someone they shouldn't have."

"Are you saying you're karma?"

"Only way to look at it. Keeps the vicious little cycle going."

"Gotta stop sometime."

"Not mine."

Kaiser finished his beer. Got up to leave. "Thanks."

"Before you go," the bartender called after him, stopping him.

The bartender smiled. "Try talking once in a while. Might loosen you up a bit."

On his way out of the parking lot, Kaiser stopped beside the row of parked motorcycles that belonged to the bikers he'd throttled in the bar—

—and kicked the side of a black Harley Davidson. The rest toppled like dominos with a resounding crash.

He crossed the road. Paid the gas station attendant. Took off in his truck, unaware that the bartender's watchful eyes were following him down the road.

As Kaiser disappeared from sight, the bartender reached for the phone...

A barn twelve kilometres up the road

The 'crackpot' snapped his cell phone shut and set it down on the table beside his rocking chair. Sitting on the front porch of his single-storey house. Chewing tobacco. Overlooking a dirt lot that culminated into a narrow, winding path that connected it to the highway. One car and two trucks were parked in a semi-circle in front of the house.

To his right stood a rickety old barn with a much newer greenhouse at the back. To his left was all open field.

The news the bartender relayed greatly disturbed him. He got up from his chair and spat his tobacco over the balcony rail as he descended the stairs. He crossed the dirt clearing to the barn. Stepped into the middle of an eight-player poker game in an otherwise empty stable. The other five stables had a seven-year supply of cocaine divided amongst them—all packaged up and neatly stacked in large crates.

A mixture of cigarette and marijuana smoke filled the barn with a faintly bluish haze and a bittersweet stench. The guys around the table were yelling and laughing at each other. Throwing cards down. Guzzling beer. Puffing smoke. All while Megadeth roared through the speakers of a stereo that had been propped on a stool at the stable entrance.

Bill watched his hired help chatter across the table, eager to win the bargaining chips piled up in the center. Then he switched off the stereo. Turned heads toward him. Everything fell silent.

"What's up, boss?" one of his goons asked.

"We've got trouble," Bill answered. "One of my old enforcers is making trouble."

"Trouble's my middle name," a short, stout enforcer said from the other side of the table.

Bill smirked at the short enforcer's ignorance regarding the seriousness of their situation. He only needed to say, "It's Kaiser Corbane."

The name slapped all confidence off their faces. A few eyes went wide as saucers. Half-smoked joints slipped out of slack-jawed mouths. They all knew Kaiser Corbane, and were all too familiar with his volatile reputation.

"W-we didn't do nothin'!" a bald enforcer exclaimed. "What the fuck's he want with us?"

"It's not us he wants," Bill said, "it's my older brother. Turns out he pissed off Kaiser Corbane. And we all know how thorough Kaiser is when it comes to this shit. He's slaughtered entire families just for their affiliations with his targets. And then burned down their homes. And then sent explosives to their offices through the mail. Imagine what he'll do to us."

"What the fuck did you brother do?" another enforcer asked nervously. "Spill wine on his foot? Leave a horse head in his bed?"

Bill stated, "My brother—in all his blissful ignorance—fucked his wife."

The enforcers' faces lit up with disbelief and horror. One of them said, "He... fucked... Kaiser Corbane's wife?"

Bill said, "Yup."

"...He fucked her fucked her?"

"That's what I said," Bill answered. Added, "On multiple

occasions, apparently."

"Shit," the short enforcer said. "We're fucked. Our operation's fucked, too. And your brother—oh, man—he's definitely fucked."

"Not if we get Kaiser first," Bill said. "I'm worried about the fate of our distribution operation, don't get me wrong. But I'm a lot more worried about my brother. I love my brother. I don't want him killed over a little honest mistake. He just moved into this town a few months ago. He doesn't know his way around, let alone the locals. He met a beautiful woman and fucked her. Only problem is that it was Kaiser Corbane's wife. Gentleman," he said with a determined twinkle in his eyes, "what we need to do is simple: take Kaiser Corbane out of the equation."

"How?!" the tallest enforcer asked. "This is Kaiser fuckin' Corbane we're talking about! How the hell are we gonna kill Kaiser Corbane?"

"The traffic cop routine," Bill said. "I want two of you on that road in five minutes. Cut him off. Stop him. Ensnare him. Then kill him." He surveyed the stable. "Any volunteers?"

"I'll go," the short one said as he pushed his way around the table.

With a hesitant sigh, the tallest enforcer quickly followed him without a word.

"Good," Bill said with a smile. "That's what I like to see." He turned to his two volunteers and said, "When you get him to stop, don't fuck around. You kill him first chance you get. If Jon doesn't survive the day, I'll be very fucking upset."

Chapter Seven: A Game of Twister

The Donovan estate—an hour later

Jim Donovan sat at the table with the morning paper and a bologna sandwich. Casually eating and reading as if it were just another quiet Sunday afternoon. And in a way, it was. He could relax. The evidence had been disposed of. Now it was just a matter of finding out who murdered Nancy Corbane in the first place. Maybe he did him in and buried him in the crop fields. Maybe they were all paranoid of a killer Jim had already disposed of. It would make sense. Two lovers caught in an affair, both with close ties to two highly dangerous criminals who just happened to be competitors as well. Classic 'Romeo and Juliet' bullshit, only Jim pulled the trigger on Jon before he could do it himself.

I bet we're all just being idiots, Jim thought as he flipped to the sports section of his paper. This scenario worked itself out.

His cell phone vibrated on the table. Jim grabbed it and flipped it open. "Hello?"

Al responded on the other end, "Evenin', bro. How far out should I drive?"

"As far as you can manage. I don't want that filing cabinet to be found for at least ten years."

"Goddamn it. Any exact ideas?"

"Where are you?"

"Approaching the suspension bridge. I might be, uh... maybe five kilometres away from the house."

"Only five? You've been driving for over an hour and you only covered a five-kilometre distance?"

"We stopped to get something to eat."

Jim fumed, "...You stopped at a restaurant... in a public place... with a bloody filing cabinet in the back of your van?"

"Yeah. Is there a problem?"

"Yes, there's a fucking problem, you blithering idiot! We have a very limited amount of time before Kaiser Corbane gets to my house!"

"So what? We've got the last of the evidence in the back."

"If he notices that there's a filing cabinet missing, he'll get suspicious, Al. And I don't want Kaiser Corbane to feel any more suspicious than he'll already be when he comes in askin' for his wife. Before you get back, I want you to make a quick pit stop at a department store and pick up an exact replica of the cabinet you buried. I want everything perfect. Aside from the potential murderer lurking in my estate, you're the final loose end. Or rather, that cabinet is, and I want you to tie it up."

"Alright, alright. It'll be—hey! Don't touch that."

Something wrong?" Jim asked.

"It's just Jeff fucking with my stereo. Sod off, you prick!"

Jeff replied in the background, "You sod off, you British bastard!"

Jim sighed as the two voices on the other end became a jumbled mess. Indecipherable bickering. It escalated to a loud ruckus. Then a deafening CLICK sounded, and the line went dead.

"Hello?" Jim said. "Hello? Al. Answer me. You there?"

Nothing. Jim snapped the phone shut and sent it sliding across the table. "Idiots."

Jim didn't have time to look at his newspaper again because Candice had suddenly burst into the kitchen. She searched frantically until she found him in the corner, one leg resting on the other. Tears pouring down her face. Body trembling. "Jim!" she shouted.

"Shh," he said, "indoor voice."

She spilled her panic all over the kitchen floor like vomit. "There's been... been...! It's bad, there's been..."

"Slow down. Keep calm... and tell me what happened."

"There's been... a murder!"

Jim stared at her. Eyebrows furrowed. Eyes narrowed with mild irritation. "No shit."

"No, I mean there's been... another murder!"

Jim blinked. "What?"

"It's Twister!" Candice sobbed. "He's...!"

"Dead." Brad shook his head slowly as he stared down at the grisly mess that used to be 'Twister' Chay. It looked as if 'Twister' had been dropped in a blender and dumped onto the carpet, which he was now soaking into. Dark red, with bits of flesh resembling raw hamburger meat strewn about; and shreds of his clothing were evident here and there. "Tsk. Tsk. Way dead." Brad took a swig from a red wine bottle he'd taken from the fridge. "Fuckin' weird. Ah've had whiskey more solid'n this poor bastard. Goddamn fine hames right here."

The others were gathered around the corpse. There weren't many of them left. Just Candice, Jim, Charley, Brad, and June. With Al and Jeff driving away with the filing cabinet—they were the only ones who weren't present who were alive, at least. Jon, Nancy, and now 'Twister' were dead. Soon they would all be dead.

"Well," June said before taking a drag from yet another cigarette. She turned to Jim and added, "You sure know how to throw a party, Jim."

Jim frowned. He knew someone would say that eventually. "It's taken an anti-clockwise turn for the worst, that's for sure."

"I wonder what you've got in store for Christmas." Despite the gruesome sight before her, June seemed partially amused.

Candice was not amused. She was busy throwing up in the farthest corner of the room.

"Jesus Christ," Charley gasped, holding a handkerchief over his mouth and nose. "What a goddamn mess. Who the fuck did this?" He turned to Brad. "You?"

"No way," Brad said. "Ah was takin' a shit with me whiskey in the jacks."

Jim scoffed. "He's too fuckin' bladdered to do anything else except destroy my toilets and drink my alcohol."

Charley whirled around, pointed at Jim. "What about you, you fuckin' scumbag? Since you've got the tendency to shoot people on a whim, I should've asked you first."

Jim gestured toward the crimson sea of mush on his floor. "When I fuck somebody up this bad with a .45, I'll let you know."

"Could've just used a different weapon."

"I could've," Jim said, "but not in my fucking house, on my bloody floor!" He pointed at the corpse. "On my five-hundred-dollar carpet!"

"Did you or didn't you?"

"No! I was in the kitchen, eating my sandwich. Reading my paper."

"Oh, really?"

"Uh," Candice spoke up. She faltered when all eyes turned to her. "H-he was in the kitchen when I looked for him."

"Eating a sandwich?" Charley asked.

Candice nodded.

Brad added, "Readin' tha paper?"

Candice nodded again. "Yes."

"Was it tha sports section?" Brad asked.

"How should I know?!" she exclaimed.

"And what about you?" Jim asked Charley. "Where were you?"

"Upstairs," Charley said.

Jim pointed at Candice. "You?"

"I-I was walking through the halls when I heard a ruckus. I went to investigate, and... and...!" her eyes darted to Twister's corpse and she started to sob. Then she turned around to puke in the corner some more.

Jim pointed at June. "And you?"

"Upstairs," she said with a playful wink.

"Right," Jim said, turning toward Candice. "And how can we possibly believe that you were—"

Suddenly it clicked. He stopped and turned around. Looked at Charley. Then at June. "You two...?"

"Oh, don't worry," June said, "we took one of the guest rooms."

Jim looked at Charley, who looked away shamefully and scratched behind his ear. Jim scoffed in disgust. "Fucking animals." He turned to Brad. "How can we know for sure that you were in the john?"

"Ah got a diabolical case o' tha runs," Brad said. His stomach growled exaggeratedly on cue. "Me arse hurts somethin' fierce. It was really... oily."

"Okay," June said, eyebrow arched, "that's a little too much information."

"Too much, but necessary," Brad said with a grin.

"Wrong," June said.

Jim pointed at Candice. "What about you?"

She looked at him, wiping vomit from her chin. "What?"

"How can we know for certain that you were in the halls? Which halls, exactly? South halls on this floor? The ground floor? The top floor? Which...?"

Brad said, "She kept knockin' on tha door, askin' if ah was okay. Like, two-minute intervals. An' we were way out on tha other side o' tha house from here."

Half an hour earlier

Brad was on the toilet, all colour drained from his face. Toilet had to be clogged by now. The thick stench that pervaded the air smelled of death itself. He groaned as he felt another batch coming. He quickly guzzled down a quarter of the wine contained in his bottle. "Oh, Jaysus!"

Candice's small fist came rapping on the other side. "Are you alright, Brad?"

"Just... fine!" he called out between dumps. Quickly flushed the toilet. He didn't want to clog it. "Aw, shit!"

Back to the present

"Yeah," Jim said, "That wasn't too much information for me to know..."

"It was brutal," Brad said.

"I get it. Blimey. You remind me of my brother. He doesn't shut up either, when it comes to stories about shit."

"Ah'm shuttin' up, alright?" Brad gulped the last of his wine and asked, "You got a recyclin' bin?"

"In the kitchen," Jim said. "That's your last bottle. Stop drinking my alcohol."

"Fuck you," Brad said as he stumbled past him to the door.

"Eat some goddamn Lucky Charms instead."

"Look who's makin' the racist jokes now, ya British fuck." And, with that, Brad was gone.

Jim shook his head with frustration clear on his face. He looked at Charley and June. "You two. I want you to explain why the hell you were fuckin' each other's brains out in my house while there's a murderer lurking about."

"Funny you mention that," June said, taking the initiative that Charley clearly didn't want to take for himself. "Because that's the exact reason why we..." she smirked, "...made love in your guest room."

"Oh," Candice said as she finally stepped out of the corner. "Wonderful. My cue to leave."

"Not you," Jim barked, pointing at her. Stopping her dead in her tracks. "You're staying, too. I want your story. Make sure you check out."

"Goddamn it, I don't want to hear about their fuck fantasy!"

Candice shouted. "I'm already feeling more sickness coming on."

"You're staying, bitch."

"Do you want me to puke all over your furniture some more?"

Jim glared at her. Then he said, "Get outta here."

"That's what I thought," she said. Then she darted out of the room, leaving the trio alone with Twister's hacked-up body strewn across the floor.

June began, "I wouldn't say it was fantasy, since it actually happened, but..." she took a drag off her cigarette before continuing, not the least bit hesitant despite what she was about to say, "...you sure you want every detail?"

Jim nodded, crossing his arms. Took a seat in a nearby armchair. "Whatever keeps you clear of suspicion."

"Oh, God," Charley muttered behind June. "Do me a favour and shoot me now."

"Don't tempt me," Jim said.

"Quiet, children," June said with a condescending, yet beautiful smile. "I've got a story to tell."

Chapter Eight: Party for Two

The Donovan estate—half an hour earlier

Charley was alone in the guest room. Seated at the edge of the bed, staring through the glass doors that led to the balcony, which overlooked the lush green backyard, the wide rectangular pool, and the luxury patio that bordered it. The sun had begun to set. The sky turned into a surreal mixture of orange and blue.

Charley glanced at his wristwatch. Five o'clock exactly. He released a heavy sigh. He was the one who convinced Jon to accompany him to the tea party when he'd received the invitation in the mailbox just three days before the day of the event. Jon refused to go at first, but Charley had coaxed him into coming along. How?

"That lovely Corbane missus will be there," he had said. And that was the selling point. It hooked Jon, and Jon would never have let go. Charley had known about the affair three months before the tea party. Being a newcomer to the township of Cherry Springs, Charley had not yet heard of Kaiser Corbane, or of his extreme reputation. He had met Nancy Corbane on two occasions, and her seemingly timid nature gave the impression that maybe, just maybe, her husband drank a little too much and was a little too rough for far too long. Charley held onto that thought. He held onto it for so long that he started to believe it to be the actual truth. It helped him justify his turning a blind eye to the affair as it slowly escalated, instead of advising Jon to let her go and stop his interference with the marriage.

"I'm sorry, Jon," Charley muttered solemnly. Took a swig from a bottle of champagne without bothering to pour it into a glass. Tears began to stream down his face. "Christ, I'm sorry. I didn't..."

He wondered if Jon really did kill her. Perhaps she told him about her husband and, in a panic, he shot her, figuring it to be the end. Maybe they had made a murder/suicide pact. Only he fled the scene before he could do himself. Jon was timid that way. He was a hopeless romantic. A fan of Shakespeare. He must have thrown the gun away and fled the scene when he heard the other partygoers reacting to the shot. If he had the nerve, he would have gone the 'Romeo and Juliet' route.

Or would he?

Charley shook his head. He didn't want his last memory of his friend being that he was a murderer, especially since this whole dilemma was possibly the result of their affair. He especially didn't want to jump to any conclusions.

A dominant, yet angelic voice cut the silence: "Is there room on that bed for two?"

Charley whirled without getting up. Saw June standing in the doorway with two wine glasses in her left hand and a fresh bottle of champagne in her right, both of which were raised like offerings. Charley's heart leaped in his throat. He gulped it down. "Miss Garden."

A playful grin crossed her doll-like face. Strangely, she was wearing little to no makeup despite her polished look. "Please," she said as she stepped into the room, "June will do. No need to be so formal."

"Alright... June... w-what can I do for you?" Charley tapped his hands on his knees restlessly as she approached the windows.

"I figured you'd like some company," she said.

"Company?"

"I've been in these situations before," she said.

"You have...?" he asked nervously as he watched her slender form drift around the foot of the bed. She was electrifying in that red dress.

"Well, perhaps not so... intense, shall we say. Brad referred to a board game. I had never been in this particular kind of situation before. But I've been involved in murder cases."

"How's that?"

"I'm a woman, Charley," she said, turning to face him. "With womanly needs. I thrive on the hilarity of bluntness and the pleasure of promiscuity. To see the looks on the faces of men when I tell them straight-up, 'You and I are going to share a room after this next drink,' to see the colour drain from the faces of these inexperienced young men... I don't know. I just find it entertaining. I humiliate them. And then I take them."

"So you're that type of woman."

"Yes, Charley. That type of woman." She bent forward. Set the glasses and the bottle down on the footlocker. Allowed Charley to see the tops of her breasts gleaming in the dulling sunlight—an opportunity that he both intentionally and unintentionally accepted with wide eyes.

"Why are you suddenly so nice?"

"I've always been nice, Charley." She turned to him. Shook her hand toward the front of the bed. "Move."

Charley quickly shifted up the bed, giving her space to sit down.

She perched herself on the edge between him and the footlocker. Poured champagne into each of the glasses until they were half full. Took one in each hand. Offered one to Charley. He took it. She sipped from the other glass. "I just find you the most interesting."

"I'd say Jim Donovan is the most interesting man here."

"Yes, but Jim Donovan is very unattractive. Personality-wise... and physically, he's appalling. How old are you, Charley?"

He hesitated. "Fifty-six." Twenty-one years older than you. Old enough to be your father, for Christ's sake.

"Huh," she said, as if surprised by his answer. "You look younger."

"No," he said with a humble smile. "Now you're flattering me."

"No, you seriously look younger."

"How much younger?"

"Try ten years. Maybe more."

He looked at her. Noticed the idle glass in his hand. Sipped from it. "Really?"

June nodded, maintaining her smile. "Yes. I must say, you've aged well, Charley."

"Well, hell. Thanks."

She eyed him carefully as he took another timid sip from his glass. "You look like a man who was deep in thought."

"Oh, it's... it's nothing."

She exhaled smoothly. Leaned toward him. "What was Charley Murphy thinking about whilst staring blissfully at the sunset?"

Charley let out a weak chuckle. "I wouldn't really call it 'blissful,' but uh... I was thinking about this whole thing. Jon and Nancy."

"Oh?" she said, drawing back. She knew where this was going.

"You see... I have this feeling that if I hadn't insisted on Jon accompanying me to this tea party... that none of this would be happening."

"You think Jon killed Corbane?"

"You don't seem too concerned..."

"My brother was an enforcer next to her husband. He told me some interesting things. I worked a few jobs with her. Small diamond jobs." June shrugged. Sipped from her glass. "She's nothing special. Certainly not worth all this trouble." She looked at him. "You didn't answer my question, Charley."

"I... I don't know. I don't want to think so. He's my best friend. Maybe it's my fault."

"How so?" she asked as she emptied her glass. Feigned sympathy. Rolled her eyes.

"I practically dragged him here. If I didn't do that, he'd still be alive. Nancy would still be alive. And Kaiser Corbane might not be on a mission to kill us all."

"Uh-huh," she said as she offered him the champagne bottle. "Refill?"

Charley took a quick glance at the bottle. Eyes gleaming. He finished his glass in two hasty gulps and held it out for more. June promptly refilled it, this time up to the brim, nearly spilling some on the white carpet. "Thank you," he said.

"Don't mention it," June replied as she refilled her own glass before setting the bottle down on the footlocker.

"That bastard," Charley said through gritted teeth. "Goddamn Jim Donovan. Shot him like a dog without coming to any sensible conclusion. Not like I'm much better."

"You feel responsible for everything, don't you?"

"As much as I hate Jim for what he did... I can't deny my involvement. I may as well have pulled the trigger myself." He gulped down a good portion of champagne. Wiped the back of his hand across his mouth. "I dragged Jon to his death."

"Please, Charley," she said as she sipped her glass with professional restraint. "Now you're being too hard on yourself."

"Am I?"

"I think so."

"I don't." He downed the rest of his glass.

She smiled. Held up the bottle again. "Enjoying yourself?"

"Why... why did you come in here, anyway?"

"I planned to get you drunk. It appears to be working."

"You wanted to get my drunk? Why...?" Despite his suspicions, Charley held up his glass for yet another refill.

June leaned closer. Her cherry-scented fragrance with a hint of the undeniable smell of cigarettes made for an interesting combination. In his current state, Charley found her scent slightly arousing. The smile on her beautiful face, and the abundant cleavage her dress provided, caused more than a startled flicker in his heartbeat. Breasts shifting delicately and freely in the bosom of her low-cut, spaghetti-string outfit.

Champagne trickled into his glass. Rose up to the brim. The whole time, Charley's eyes were inadvertently fixed on her chest. Trance-like. She knew what she was doing.

June glanced up as he brought the glass to his lips. A sip. A gulp. In no time he was chugging the glass like a college student. "You asked 'why,'" she said, shrugging. Straightened and set the bottle back on the footlocker. "I'd like to get my mind off this. I figured someone else might, too."

"Brad's already drunk. If that was what you mean..."

"Brad's always drunk," she said. "I have no interest in that kind of man."

"A drunk?"

"No. A man who doesn't know the definition of the word 'restraint.' It's more fun to peel away the restraints that hold back uptight men like yourself."

"Oh... look..."

Incoming speech. She caught it right away and stood up.

"Y-you're a very beautiful woman," Charley said. "I can see that clear as day. B-but there are things I wouldn't feel right doing. In this situation... I mean, my best friend was just killed because of me a few hours earlier today. I don't think—"

Before he could continue, June's gloved fingers hooked under her dress strings and lifted them off her shoulders. Her dress slipped to the floor. Ample, teardrop breasts fully visible. Black laced panties. Bare feet dipped in high heels. The sight dropped his jaw. Speech lost and long forgotten.

"Oh. My sincerest apologies," she said casually, lighting herself another cigarette. Took a quick drag. Blew smoke in his direction. "Did I interrupt you?"

He gawked at her for a good minute. Empty glass slipped through his fingers and landed on the soft carpet without a sound.

Wide eyes ogled her as she stepped out of her shoes.

Paralyzed under Medusa's cold stare.

She placed her hands on his chest. Red velvet palms gliding across his shirt. Forcing him gently on his back. Eager hands supporting a woman who knew how to climb on top of a man while being light as a feather. Straddling him. Buttons coming undone. Belt buckle falling open.

His hands gripping her thighs. Panty strings coming undone. Trousers falling to the floor. Lustful energy getting hotter by the second. Skin grinding on skin. Velvet gloves coming off and fluttering to the foot of the bed like ribbons. His large hands greedily cupping her breasts.

A dominant, slender figure pinned down her new servant—one who was more than happy to comply to her every demand. Heavy breathing. Long sighs. A pleasurable moan piercing the air. Arched back. Breasts high, out of his reach. Hips grinding—

Present

"Heard enough?" June asked, not the least bit embarrassed. "Or do you want me to describe, in great detail, the three times I made him cum?"

Charley's face was redder than a stop sign. He sputtered, "That's enough. Thank you."

Jim stared at her, not quite transfixed by her alluring presence, and not quite horrified about the potential state he'd see his freshly clean sheets in. But like she'd said before—at least it was the guest room. "You bonked him to get your mind off things?"

"Well, his, too, I suppose..."

Jim looked at Charley, who didn't dare look up. He shook his head and said, "Get the fuck outta here."

"With pleasure," June said. On her way out, she grabbed Charley by the wrist and pulled him with her. "Come on. I'm not done with you yet."

Chapter Nine: Traffic Cops

Kaiser Corbane

He had not shown up to this particular section of the road just yet. Two men disguised as traffic cops were crouched in the ditch awaiting his arrival. The shorter one held the stop sign on a pole, standing it up like a sentry on guard. The taller one kept looking down both ends of the seemingly endless stretch of road. The wind blew softly, rustling the billions of corn stalks that stood mightily on either side of the road. The crop fields also carpeted the rolling hills as far as their eyes could see. In the distance, a cow mooed. Up above, a crow cawed.

"Kaiser fuckin' Corbane," Tall Cop muttered. "This is suicide."

"Tell me about it." Short Cop scoffed. "First chance we get: pop! We put one through his forehead."

"Yeah, and another five in his face for good measure." Tall Cop paused. Shrugged. "Two more in his chest just to be sure." He drew his revolver from the holster under his vest. Gripped it with both hands and pointed it at the gravel, pretending that one of the larger pebbles was Kaiser Corbane's head. "Wouldn't know what hit him."

"Put the gun away," Short Cop said. "I'm already on edge as it is. Seeing you wave that giant fucking cannon around like the national flag on the eve of a revolution doesn't help."

"I'll have you know this is a goddamn classic," Tall Cop said as he held up the revolver for his partner to behold. Smith & Wesson Model 500. Shiny silver glint. Thick. Big. Powerful. Truly a giant fucking cannon. "Every shot fired is like riding an angry bull with a red blindfold on. One slug from this thing could stop Superman in his tracks better than Kryptonite."

"Uh-huh."

"Unimpressed, huh? Let's see your piece."

"No."

"Come on, take it out. Don't be shy."

"Okay, now you've made it weird."

"C'mon," Tall Cop pushed. "We're both men here."

With an annoyed sigh, Short Cop reached under his vest. Brought out a Beretta 92SB pistol for Tall Cop to see. Blued steel. Dwarfed in comparison to his partner's revolver. "There. Satisfied?"

Tall Cop nodded with approval. "It's a good gun, I'll admit. Doesn't compare, though."

"Yeah, yeah." Short Cop holstered his gun. "Shut up."

Tall Cop looked at the stop sign in his partner's hand. "You ever hit a guy with one of those?"

Short Cop looked at the stop sign he wielded. Shook his head. "Nah, man. I don't think I've ever actually held one of these before. This is my first time as a 'traffic cop.' You?"

"Lopped a guy's head off with one of those. A real traffic cop, in fact."

"You don't say?"

"Yeah," Tall Cop said, nodding. "Swung it like... like an axe. A battle axe. I didn't hit him with the flat part of it. That'd just break his face, maybe."

"Oh, I get it now. Thought you were bullshitting me for a second. But you hit him with the edge."

Tall Cop nodded. "Hit him with the edge. Right through the fuckin' neck."

"What's it like to behead a guy with a stop sign?"

"Like... like..." Tall Cop said, pondering how to describe the experience, "...like cutting a huge knife through a giant sausage."

"Giant sausage," Short Cop repeated.

"A nice, big, Oktoberfest sausage," Tall Cop said, flashing a toothy grin at the corn stalks across the road.

They stopped talking after that. Listened to the wind whistle through the corn stalk walls.

The silence was short-lived.

Short Cop said, "I'm hungry."

"Deal with it," Tall Cop said.

"Diner's just a couple kilometres up the road."

"Bill told us to wait for him and kill him, so we're gonna wait for him and kill him. I've seen what he does to people who leave their posts. Doesn't matter what the reason is; the punishment's the same"

"What if he doesn't show?"

"He'll show."

"Yeah, but what if he doesn't?"

"He'll show," Tall Cop assured him.

"What if he took a back road? We'd be standing out here all night."

"That right there is how I know you're not from around here," Tall Cop said, annoyed. "In this particular stretch of farmland, there are no back roads. It's just this highway. Every alternative dirt road you think you'll find ends up revealing itself as a driveway to some farmer's house."

"Could be one you missed."

"I've been going up and down this road as Bill's enforcer for twenty years. There isn't a single driveway I haven't been on. Trust me. There ain't any back roads up here."

"You sure?"

"Positive. Now be quiet. I think I hear something."

They raised their heads and listened. Looked to the east. Sure enough, the wind carried the unmistakable droning sound of a truck's engine. They couldn't see anything over the peak of the hill yet.

"Think it's our guy?" Short Cop asked.

"Let's hope so," Tall Cop answered, eyeing the hill intently.

The peak of the hill shimmered like an oasis under the sun. In seconds, a red dot hatched from its top and come down like a shining droplet. As it approached, its features became more comprehensive. The silver grill. The windshield. The dull red paintjob.

Once the pickup truck was within fifty yards of the fake traffic cops' location, Short Cop stepped onto the road, held up his stop sign, and waved at the undetermined driver.

Tall Cop stood back and observed, waiting for the truck to slow down.

It didn't.

The pickup struck Short Cop down and blew past Tall Cop, leaving him dumbfounded. Stop sign clattered a few feet away. Short Cop was now road kill.

Kaiser Corbane flinched, acting surprised when a streak of blood and brains splattered across the windshield. "Fucking mosquitoes," he quipped. Turned on the windshield wipers.

"Jesus Christ!" Tall Cop gasped. Rooted to the spot for only a moment, he whirled and scrambled down the slope, disappeared into the crops. Came back out seconds later in a Jeep. Vaulted out of the ditch. Hit the road. Swerved. Burning rubber as it charged in pursuit of the truck. "You fucking cocksucker!"

Kaiser drove on, unperturbed that he had just flattened an apparent traffic cop, and was now being pursued by his partner. He was mildly amused at the thought that Bill Whitby actually believed he could ensnare him with one of his regular traps. Kaiser had known the bastard for six years, and he knew every trick the man had up his sleeve. "Never use regular enforcers to catch an ex-enforcer," Kaiser said, to no one in particular. He chuckled as he switched on the radio. "Stupid asshole."

Tall Cop was closing the gap between him and Kaiser Corbane. An endless stream of profanities tumbling out of his mouth as he floored the accelerator. Turned into the opposite lane. Came up beside Kaiser's truck. Shouted through the passenger window as he drew his revolver from under his brightly coloured vest. "You motherfucker, you flattened my partner! I'll fucking gut you, you hear me?! I'll fucking..."

Kaiser looked at him. Window was up. Johnny Cash was playing on the radio. He couldn't hear a damn thing Tall Cop was saying. Instead, he smiled and waved, feigning innocence to an enforcer burning with manic rage.

Tall Cop fired. Revolver bucked concussively. Blew out the passenger window. Slug punched into the truck's door and harmlessly zipped under Kaiser's seat. Another shot—the bullet glanced off the hood and sent shallow cracks rippling across the windshield. Another shot—

Kaiser floored the brake. The truck slewed back. Kaiser spun the wheel. The truck smashed into the Jeep's tail. Hurled it into an out-of-control 360. Kaiser gunned it. The truck broadsided the Jeep in mid-spin and sent it flying off its wheels. The Jeep tumbled down the road, hood over taillight, flinging metal into the air. Rolled off into the ditch. Crushed its way through a row of corn stalks. Did one last roll before settling on its roof.

Kaiser taxied to the gravel curb. Got out. Walked over to the top of the ditch to observe his latest work. The Jeep was battered beyond recognition, windows blown out, the three remaining tires jutting up crookedly.

Kaiser turned to see the last tire wobbled further down the road. Solo act. He watched it go on by itself before it inevitably keeled over on its side.

A pained groan drew Kaiser's cold eyes back to the wrecked Jeep in the ditch. Tall Cop was gradually crawling out through the shattered windshield. Still clutching his revolver. Blood streaming down his head from four different places. One of his eyes were closed, most likely from having his face slammed into the dashboard. He looked up at Kaiser and spat, "You... fucker!"

Kaiser shrugged. Casually descended the slope.

Tall Cop strained to lift his gun.

Kaiser was upon him in no time, stomping his foot down on his gun-wielding hand. Tall Cop howled in pain as he felt his finger bones pop under Kaiser's weight. "FUCK!"

Kaiser squatted and took the revolver away. "I'd been expecting you. What took you so long?"

"Fuck you!" Tall Cop growled.

Patiently, Kaiser pressed the barrel of the Model 500 against Tall Cop's forehead. "Your boss is an idiot. Bill ought to have known better than to try old tactics on me. It's like he wanted me to kill you and your fuckhead partner. In that case, the job's half done already." He cocked the hammer back with his thumb. "Now if I didn't know better... I'd say Bill would like to speak with me. Most likely concerning the matter of his brother fucking my wife. Am I close?"

"Not even close," Tall Cop hissed through gritted, bloody teeth. "He wants you out."

"Out, eh?"

"Off this track. Outta this town. Doesn't want you to kill his brother."

"I guess it was inevitable. Siblings gotta stick together, right?" And, with that, Kaiser stood up and fired. Tall Cop's head fragmented and blew upwards like a science fair volcano.

Chapter Ten: Clue Hunt

Donovan estate

Jim returned to the kitchen to find Brad seated at the table with a fresh can of a beer. Staring off into space. Jim's patience was running thin. "I told you to stop drinking my booze."

Snapping out of his apparent trance, Brad's head jerked in his direction. He slurred, "What?"

As Jim made his way to the island in the middle of the kitchen, where he had thrown his newspaper earlier, he said, "Keep drinking my alcohol and pretty soon I'll be charging you twenty bucks a can. Fifty a bottle."

"That's not fair."

"Life's not fair. Just count yourself lucky I'm not chargin' you for the alcohol you already sucked up today. The bloody larder's gotta be half as stocked as it used to be by now."

Brad shrugged. "Maybe... I dunno." A pause. "Wasn't really payin' attention."

"Uh-huh."

Brad hiccupped. Beer sprayed from the jolted can in his hand and got on the vest of his suit. Brad looked at the fresh stains and said, "Aaaww... now ah gotta get me other suit..."

"You mean you have more than one o' those hideous things? Euch!"

"Don't knock tha suit," Brad snapped.

Jim scowled. "You don't seem too worried about these murders," he said, eyes narrowed with suspicion. "In fact, you seem more worried 'bout your suit than the general loss o' life in this house."

"In me defense, Ah'm..." he belched before finishing, "...paralytic."

"Good point." Jim turned and headed out the door. "Sit tight, then."

Investigative work was something Jim was good at. He was the most observant of the three Donovan siblings, and neither one of his brothers could pull wool over his eyes.

First thing he looked for was a weapon. He looked in the basement cabinet where he hid the Desert Eagle. There it sat in the top drawer, undisturbed, sharing the sealed plastic bag with the spent shell casing. He closed the cabinet drawer and locked it. He knew a Desert Eagle couldn't have possibly left Twister Chay in the state he was found in. His check-up was more of a precaution to make sure no one had stolen it for future purposes.

Jim made damn sure the Desert Eagle was safe. And then he checked the locks that kept the small arms storage compartment on the other side of the basement airtight. Like all members in his family, Jim Donovan had his own secret arms cache. A good precautionary tradition that ran in the family.

He was looking for a big knife, or a machete, or something else that could hack up Twister Chay like that.

Or rather, he was deliberately looking for what wasn't there. He knew where his maid Sandra put everything, so if something was missing, he would know.

Jim went upstairs to the main floor. Made sure the other guests weren't around before sneaking out the back door of his house onto the patio. The property was four acres; all green grass with a few oak trees, the swimming pool, and a tool shed sitting isolated behind the garden at the far end of the backyard. All enclosed within a five-foot-tall brick wall.

He rounded the pool. Stole constant glances over his shoulder for any eyes that could be staring through the windows. Stumbled halfway. Nearly fell into the pool. Swore and regained his footing at the last second. Stood up straight. Looked around again, then, satisfied no one had noticed him, he continued across the yard.

Circled an oak. Jumped the flowerbed. Broke into a run for the tool shed.

He didn't have to reach it to see that the padlock had been broken off the latch. Once he did reach it, Jim hissed, "Shit," and kicked the door open. It swung inward, bounced off a tool shelf.

Jim stomped inside, eyes darting back and forth, from shelf to shelf. Chainsaw. Toolbox. Rake. Shovel. The missing saw, which had been used to cut up Nancy Corbane. A rusty ax that had mysteriously vanished. Bingo.

At this point, Jim had forgotten about the ax he had Brad retrieve during the dismemberment process of Nancy Corbane's body. The man was trying so hard to find the little things that he ended up forgetting about the other things. In this situation, in his state of mind, can you blame him?

Next: all the closets in the house. No one could hack up a body without getting some blood on their clothes, but everyone who had gathered around Twister's body was as clean as they were when they first arrived at the estate that morning—with the exception being Brad, but that was due to the additional alcohol stains on his hideous orange suit. And to Jim, that could only mean one thing...

After the broom closet and his personal walk-in closet in his bedroom, Jim sifted through the coats on the rack in the foyer closet. It didn't take him long to discover that a raincoat was missing. An old yellow raincoat.

He didn't need to find it. He only needed to find out who took it. Charley? June? They were off the hook... unless their story was all a lie. Brad? Too drunk to be this clever.

That just leaves Candice. Were her hands really clean? She threw up at the crime scene. That may not have meant much... but she didn't throw up when everyone found Nancy Corbane lying on the ballroom floor with her brains scattered all over.

Jim had seen several people throw up after a recent death—because they were the ones who killed them in the first place. Jim had thrown up immediately after making his first kill in 1983. The guilt choked him up. Gagged him. Before he knew it, he was hurling his lunch all over the floor over a scumbag that had broken into their house and crawled through their window. The fucker wore black, head to toe. Held a lock pick but it looked like a knife. The lighting was poor. And Jim had his father's revolver...

It was a matter of self-defense. Nothing more.

Candice wasn't defending herself. Or was she? Perhaps she was reacting the same way Jim reacted on that day. Maybe she couldn't stop herself from throwing up. Maybe she'd made her first kill. And if that were the case, that meant that she didn't kill Nancy Corbane. So who killed Nancy Corbane?

Jim didn't want to jump to conclusions just yet.

Then, suddenly, it hit him. Jim didn't know how he could have been this stupid.

Mentally, he went through the scene where he assigned everyone with their own tasks during the disposal of Nancy Corbane's body. That would explain why the ax and the raincoat were missing. Jim used both of them—and the saw—to break up Nancy's body into little pieces to make for easier transport. No one else had access to the raincoat—which was the only coat missing from Jim's collection—and the ax, except...

June and Candice—when they loaded the Tupperware container they were stored in into the back of the van. Both of them just moved up to 'prime suspect' status. And both suspects were still alive.

Jim went into his office to retrieve a third M1911 pistol from his desk drawer to replace the one he'd given to his brother earlier. He saw this situation as a battle royale that hadn't yet reached boiling point, but when it did... he'd be ready.

Jim rapped his knuckles on the guest room door. Called out, "Charley. June."

No answer.

"Quit fuckin' each other's bollocks out for a second and answer me."

Silent response.

"I'm comin' in if you don't answer."

Nothing.

"Right. In I go." Jim opened the door. The guest room was empty. A total mess, but empty. The bed was torn up. Bits of glass, some dark, some clear, were scattered all over the floor. The glass doors leading to the balcony were smashed open. There were fresh red stains in the carpet that formed a trail to the bathroom.

Nearly stopped his goddamn heart.

"What the bloody fuck?"

Jim took out one of his pistols and cautiously entered the room. Gun poised, he crossed the room, careful not to step on any glass. Stepped through the shattered doors onto the balcony. Looked over the railing at the swimming pool below. No sign of life anywhere in the backyard. But what he did find...

...was the faint, oasis-like object at the bottom of the poor. Jim leaned over the railing, peering into the pool. Only then did he realize that the L-shaped object was the missing ax.

Jim turned to the bathroom. Its door ajar, but hiding whatever the blood trail led to. Jim slowly approached. Tense. Heart pounding. He kicked the door slightly. Retracted his foot quickly as if he were about to lose it. The hinges creaked eerily as the door slowly spun in...

...Revealing Charley in his boxers. Sprawled out on the white ceramic floor in a sea of blood. Head propped on the bathtub ledge. Fresh cuts running across his face, neck, and chest. More blood oozing from the two stab wounds in his stomach.

Looked dead. Wasn't dead. His voice nearly made Jim leap out of his skin. "She did it. She... fucking stabbed me!" He broke down into a fresh sob. Panicked. As frantic as a stab victim who lost too much blood possibly could be. "Didn't see it coming. That bottle. Glass hurt like hell... the knife..."

Jim knelt down beside him, careful to keep out of range of the blood pool on the floor. "June did this? June's the fucking murderer?!"

"Using... other shower... washing away evidence..." The old man was dozing off.

"Hey!" Jim slapped him across the cheek. "Stay awake. Tell me who did this. June did this? It's June, right?"

Charley wheezed. Strained, but managed to raise his other fist, revealing a shred of yellow rubber. "Coat..." He went limp. Head lolled to the side.

Jim caught Charley's hand by the wrist before it could hit the floor and stared at the yellow shred caught in his fingers. The raincoat. "Goddamn it!"

He bolted upright and charged out of the room.

Gun in hand, Jim briskly charged down the corridor until he came upon the main bathroom door. Checked the handle. Locked. He put his ear to the door. He could hear the shower running. That bitch really was washing the evidence away.

No time to waste.

Jim kicked his foot. The door splintered, crashed to the floor in pieces. He stormed inside. Turned to the shower on the other side of the bathroom.

And there she was, standing behind the foggy, frosted glass shower doors. A slender, peach-coloured shape made even hazier by the steam. The occasional glimmer of light reflecting off fine, wet skin.

"You ain't hiding shit from us, you murderin' cunt!" Jim roared. Levelled the pistol. Fired. Glass curtains crystallized. She cried out in horror. Another shot. The glass splintered. The peach-coloured shape jerked. Another bullet blew through the glass curtains. Another hazy spasm. Faint droplets of dark red from within.

Quick succession time. Jim unloaded the rest of his clip into the shower. Glass shattered. An artery exploded. The glass dramatically changed from gleaming silver to deathly crimson. A shrill, panicked scream. Peach limbs flailing, striking out patches of glass, snapping weak gold framing. Screaming. Blood splattering. Glass spraying. Steam escaping its former confines, breaking free. Screaming. Showerhead gunning her corpse with jets of hot water.

Silence. Only the running water made noise.

Jim approached his latest kill with hollow footsteps. Sweaty grip on the empty pistol. Leaned forward. Peered through the wrecked glass doors. Water pounding a still, leathery carcass. Washing the blood away as quickly as it came. Pink water swirling down the drain.

He suddenly lurched away. Staggered back in shock. Gun slipping through rigid fingers, clattering to the floor. "Jesus—"

Candice.

Chapter Eleven: Showdown at Murphy's Barn

Bill Murphy's barn

Kaiser Corbane didn't waste any time getting to the barn. He drove the truck up the winding driveway into the dirt lot. To his total lack of surprise, he found himself approaching a three-car barricade with the rest of Bill's enforcers squatting behind it, weapons poised and ready to fire. He stopped at the peak of the hill on the edge of the lot.

Got out. Giant fucking cannon in hand. He didn't stray too far from the truck, knowing that a gun battle was pretty much inevitable at this point. Both sides of this confrontation knew how it was going to end. Whatever negotiations Bill might attempt would just be him grasping at straws, and both parties knew it.

Bill stepped out from behind the screen door of his house with a shotgun at his side. Descended the steps of his porch wearing an unconvincingly smug grin as he approached the advantageous side of the barricade. He was confident in one thing, at least: that the six enforcers taking beads on Kaiser would at least hit him once.

"Kaiser," Bill shouted across the lot, "it's been a while."

"Attempting to negotiate with me is pointless, Bill," Kaiser said.

"Always so straightforward," Bill said. "You know, I'd hate to shoot up an old friend. It'd be like shooting up family."

"You weren't my friend—you were my employer. You certainly weren't part of my family." Kaiser's angry expression contorted into a mocking smirk. "When I work for you for shitty wages, I'm your expendable grunt. But when you want something... oh. Suddenly we're friends. Hell, we're family."

"That hurts, Corbane," Bill said.

"I haven't even started dishing out the pain yet, Bill." Kaiser thumbed back the hammer on his revolver. "Not just yet."

Realizing absolutely nothing could sway his visitor, Bill said, "Can't you make an exception, just this once?"

"About your brother?"

"Yeah. Of course."

"No."

"Why the hell not?"

"He fucked my wife."

"Come on, Kaiser," Bill said with a nervous chuckle, "be reasonable. You know how many friends I have? How much money I've got? I'm sure we can come to some kinda settlement. I'd much rather we conclude this like gentlemen instead of ending it like savages."

"That ship had already left port when you decided to send two of your 'traffic cops' my way," Kaiser said. "I don't know why you thought using an old enforcer trick would work."

"It's worked before, believe it or not. You're not the first ex-enforcer to start kicking shit in places it doesn't belong."

"No, but I'll be the last."

"Yeah—"

"You have two options, Bill," Kaiser began impatiently, "you can give your brother up without a hitch, and in return I'll leave you with your operation in good standing... and the use of two of your limbs. Or you can die defending your brother—a notion that, while commendable, will result in the slaughter of your men and the destruction of all of your hard-earned possessions. By the time I'm done with you, there would be nothing left. If I were you, I'd pick the former option. I don't have the time nor the patience to go with the latter."

"Oh, really?" Bill challenged.

"It's been a long and trying day," Kaiser said. "But I'm still running with half a gallon of rage in my tank."

Bill shook his head. The smile had vanished from his face. "Always the fucking tough guy. If you kill all my guys, I'll just cut you down myself."

Kaiser's eyes narrowed. "You don't have the balls."

Bill replied, "I've got balls to spare. Just you wait an' see."

"Last chance."

"Mercy from the Kaiser Corbane?" Bill laughed. "I'm touched."

"Are those your last words?"

Bill scoffed. But before he could blink, Kaiser had already thrown up the revolver. The deafening roar. The concussive buck. Bald Enforcer's shiny head blasting off into space. Brains splattering Bill's jeans.

"Jesus!" Bill screamed. His cockiness gone with Baldy's

brains. "Holy shit! Kill him!"

Kaiser dived behind the wheel of his pickup as the remaining five enforcers blasted the truck with their shotguns. Keeping his head low, Kaiser floored the accelerator. The windows blew inward as the truck lurched forward, peeled into oncoming fire. Metal screamed as the enforcers' shot strafed the front and sides of the truck, but it stayed on its course.

Straight for the house.

In a panic, Bill aimed his shotgun and blasted a hole through the windshield. Ejected an empty shell. Fired. Nailed one of the headlights. "Shit!"

The truck suddenly swerved to the right—Bill's left—and tailgated one of the cars. Knocked it out of the way. Hard enough to send two enforcers flying. The truck pitched forward, crunching one of the fallen enforcers under its tires.

To the barn. Better yet, the greenhouse.

Bill's realization lit his face up like a jack-o'-lantern. Horrified as—

—Kaiser sent the truck blasting through the greenhouse wall. Blowing through the marijuana jungle in an explosion of glass and dirt. Sparks flew. Soil sprayed. Overhead lights folded under a shattering glass roof, dousing marijuana leaves with electrical fire. Thick marijuana foliage flattened under a raging metal beast. The truck rammed into Bill's personal grower, a fat guy in a beekeeper outfit for an unknown reason, and sent him sprawling in midair. The pot grower crashed through the opposite wall. Fell head-over-heels down the embankment on the other side of the greenhouse in a shower of glass.

The greenhouse was like a container for what was inside—and the plant life inside had grown out of control. High enough to bend under the ceiling. A thick jungle of weed, tens of thousands of dollars worth under fluorescent lights. Bordered by a few barrels of kerosene.

Now Kaiser was driving a truck through it all.

"NO!" Bill roared. Uncontrollable rage exploding. "Fucking son of a bitch!" He turned to his enforcers, frantically pointing at the greenhouse. "Kill him, for fuck's sake!"

Kaiser put the gears in reverse. Backed up. The truck hit the barn wall. Splintered it. Kept going, plowing through the stables, destroying stacks of cocaine in violent bursts of white. Wood and straw flying. Poker table toppling. Radio smashing.

Kaiser looked through the spiderwebbed windshield, back into the greenhouse. Another enforcer emerged from the thick veil of pot leaves. Fired his shotgun at the truck. Kaiser ducked as another portion of the windshield collapsed into his lap. Throttled the gas. Truck slammed forward, back into the greenhouse.

Alarmed, the enforcer scrambled back the way he came. The truck followed his movements. Then the terrified enforcer tried the other option, racing for the hole in the glass wall the grower had been thrown through. No dice. The truck swerved to match his every move.

The enforcer screamed helplessly. The truck flung him across its hood like a ragdoll. Face pressed against the windshield, the enforcer screamed, trying to get his shotgun through the holes. The truck bounced, causing the enforcer to fire haphazardly, shredding the passenger seat. Kaiser put his revolver up to the windshield and fired. Liquidized the enforcer's head in a second. Made a heavy need for windshield wipers.

The last two enforcers stood outside, blasting their shotguns through the greenhouse windows, following the truck as it rampaged to the other end of the greenhouse. All while Bill screamed into a cell phone near the porch of his house.

Kaiser vaulted through the other end. More glass flying. Headless enforcer tumbling off the hood and down the embankment. Slewed, spraying dirt. Roared back into the dirt lot, aiming for the last two enforcers.

One of them turned tail and fled. The other stood his ground, blasting at the oncoming truck. Gouged out the other headlight. Splintered even more of the windshield.

Truck picked up speed. Now the enforcer was worried. Backed up. Found himself pressing his back against the side of the car Kaiser had swiped out of his way earlier. Desperate, he aimed for Kaiser's head. Fired.

Kaiser ducked. The headrest blew apart.

The truck smashed into the enforcer. Crunched him into the side of the car. Shattered the lower half of his body. A spray of blood burst from the gargling enforcer's mouth before he crumpled over the truck's engine.

Kaiser didn't back up.

The roar of a shotgun made his eardrums pop. A load of shot

pelted the door. Snapped off the handle. Kaiser immediately replied with his revolver pointed out the passenger window. Blasted the last enforcer off balance and sent him staggering. Gun jerked violently in his hand. The slug tore a big chunk of flesh out of the bastard's shoulder. Kaiser followed up with another shot. The last slug whistled across the lot and pierced the enforcer's ribcage. Slammed him to the dirt.

Kaiser looked around from inside the truck. The lot seemed empty now. A large fire had begun to spread through the greenhouse, destroying everything Bill Murphy had grown.

Speaking of whom, there was no sign of Bill Murphy anywhere. Kaiser figured he'd retreated back into the house. He checked the cylinder of his revolver. Two bullets left. Tall Cop only had six bullets on him, not including the two left over from their encounter on the highway. He saved those, at least. Took out the empty shells. Pushed the two spares into the cylinder. Snapped the cylinder back into place.

He got out of the truck. Glanced over at the greenhouse as the flames spread, gradually melting the glass roof it blazed under. Then he reached into the rear bed of his pickup and lifted out a gasoline canister. Carried it into the barn, and started splashing it all over the smashed stables and the thick blanket of cocaine. Emptied the canister at the barn entrance. Discarded it with a half-assed toss. Lit a match. Flicked it five feet away. Returned to his pickup as the barn went up in flames. Extracted yet another gas canister from the back. Headed over to the house.

"Jesus. Oh, Jesus. Jesus. Jesus. Jesus!"

Bill Murphy panicked inside his home. He'd been gathering all the guns he had, occasionally glancing out the windows to see what Kaiser Corbane was up to. Rage and terror made his body shake uncontrollably. By the time Kaiser started for the house, Bill had his collection of rifles on the kitchen table with only half of them loaded up and ready to go.

Bill took an AK-47. Punched window glass onto the porch. Shouted through the opening, "Get the fuck off my property!" and opened up with a full-auto burst.

Kaiser ducked his head as bullets stitched across the dirt lot around him. Dived for the porch. Bullets tore the railing to splinters above his head. He remained in a squat as he made his way around the porch, splashing the porch with gasoline as he moved. Then he went to the side of the house. Gas canister in his right hand; revolver in his left. He stopped before he could reach the cellar doors. Lit a match.

Bill reloaded his AK and leaned further out the window, trying to spot Kaiser. When he couldn't see him, he blasted the floorboards of his porch to sawdust. When the porch suddenly burst into flames, he broke into a cold sweat.

He just lost sight of the most dangerous man in town—and the bastard was trapping him in a circle of fire.

"Shit. Where the fuck are you?"

Kaiser didn't reply as he made his way to the rear patio with a straw doormat. Kaiser didn't crack a smile during his moment of victory. Instead he splashed the walls, the door, the mat, and the surrounding dirt with gasoline until the canister was half full. Lit another match. Dropped it on the mat. Instant bonfire. No escape.

Bill screamed, "Where the fuck are you?! Kaiser!"

Kaiser still didn't answer. He could hear the man screaming from the side of the house, which had only one window with the blinds down. Kaiser approached the entrance to the cellar. Yanked the doors open one at a time. Climbed down the stairs. Disappeared.

Frantic, Bill scrambled from one end of the house to the other. Constantly checked the windows. Desperate in his search for Kaiser. Nowhere outside of his home was safe.

Kaiser sauntered across the cellar, which was mostly empty, with a few shelves displaying boxes full of chemicals being the only exception. He could hear Bill's running footsteps slamming on the floorboards above his head. A new layer of dust fluttered to the concrete floor with every step.

Bill kept on screaming. "You think you can threaten my brother's life and get away with it? Fuck you! Fuck you, Kaiser Corbane! You can fuck up my business! You can kill the help! But you don't fuck with my family! You have a score to settle, you settle it with me!"

He raced to the next window. Looked out. Reckless. Eyes wild. Darting around the area. Searching. He discovered the cellar doors were wide open and yelled, "Shit!"

That was his cue.

Kaiser raised his revolver and launched a slug through the

floorboards. Snapped the board in half. Blew Bill's right knee to pieces.

Bill screeched in agony. Collapsed to the floor. Assault rifle clattering nearby. "You fucking coward! Fuck! My leg! Jesus Christ! Oh, God... Christ... my goddamn leg! Fuck!"

Another shot. Bill watched in horror as his bowels erupted from his stomach. His shouting died down to a high-pitched whine and a pathetic sob. Rigid fingers feeling through the gaping hole in his stomach. Seeing if this was real or just a bad dream. All numb. Surreal. A bad dream.

Kaiser went to work. Knocked over shelves until the chemicals and building materials were spread all over the floor in an ankle-deep flood. A foul-smelling mixture of flammables and toxics. Kaiser threw in the half-empty canister for good measure. Watched it bounce off a metal shelf and splash into the dark green sea. Lit a match. Started up the stairs. Waited until he was at the top of the staircase before tossing the match inside. He dodged the fireball that immediately sprang up from inside the cellar.

In a split second, the entire basement was a flaming pit. Belching black, toxic smoke through the cracks between the floorboards. Filling the rest of the house. Choking whatever life Bill had left.

Then... a droning sound in the distance. That familiar rhythmic beat...

Kaiser stopped and looked to the west to see...

...a helicopter flying nap-of-the-earth over the crops with only one passenger—another enforcer with an M16 assault rifle equipped with a scope and a grenade launcher perched on the side. Aviator sunglasses. Dressed to kill. The man seemed to be in a hurry, because he started firing as soon as Kaiser's head became more than just a blur.

Kaiser ducked behind the middle barricade car. Bullets splintered its windshield and glanced off the hood.

The helicopter descended on the lot. The sniper loosed a full-auto burst on the car Kaiser hid behind. Blew out its tires and windows. In no time, the assault rifle had run dry. The sniper prepped the grenade launcher.

Kaiser bolted for the fiery barn, which was falling to pieces.

A grenade screamed into the lot and smashed through the car's sunroof. The concussive blast ripped the car apart. Kaiser went flying in a hail of shrapnel. Rolled in the dirt with the wind knocked out of him and a piece of hot metal sticking out of his right arm.

Kaiser groaned and returned fire with the revolver. Missed the sniper's head only by a couple inches.

The sniper signaled the pilot. The helicopter banked over the house and began circling the barn, allowing the sniper to reload without getting shot.

As the helicopter disappeared behind the barn, Kaiser got up and made a break for it. He ripped the piece of shrapnel out of his arm and flung it away as he ran. Once he made it inside the barn, he checked the cylinder of his revolver. Only one bullet left. Kaiser cursed under his breath and snapped the wheel back into place, waiting for the helicopter to reappear again.

Gas-fuelled flames raged in the flattened stables behind Kaiser, belching smoke into the rafters. Kaiser held his hand over his mouth and nose to protect his lungs from the smoke, constantly glancing upward at the flaming trusses that threatened to give out under his head.

The helicopter came around and slowed to a hover above the lot. The sniper scanned the area for his prey, assault rifle shifting with his gaze.

Kaiser, hidden behind a support beam in the barn with a clear shot. He aimed the revolver. Concentrated as best he could with the smoke providing a thin veil.

Fired.

The slug whistled through the air. Flew wide. Blew in the side window behind the pilot's head instead.

Tipped off, the sniper opened up on the barn. Kaiser took cover behind the post as bullets raked across the floor and the stables. The grenade followed, whooshed through the air. Blasted the outer wall and two crushed stables to flaming splinters.

The helicopter started its routine again. Banked over Bill Murphy's house, which was spewing black chemical smoke from every opening now. Started circling around the barn again. The routine seemed like a lucky break.

Now!

Kaiser dashed out of the barn entrance and ran along the side toward the blazing greenhouse. Grabbed hold of a kerosene barrel. Pushed it on its side.

The sniper slapped a new clip home as the helicopter made its way around the other side of the barn.

Kaiser spotted an Ingram M10 abandoned in the dirt a few paces away from a dead enforcer.

The sniper pushed a new grenade into the launcher.

The helicopter rounded the barn.

Kaiser pushed the kerosene barrel across the path. Kicked, launched it. The barrel bouncing into the cellar.

The sniper opened up on his prey.

Kaiser charged down alongside the barn, snatching up the Ingram as he went. The sniper's volley pursued him, tearing across the barn wall.

The kerosene barrel sprang off the cellar staircase into the flaming chemical sea.

The sniper ran dry. Fired the grenade.

Kaiser dived into the new hole in the wall as another grenade made it even wider. A blast of splinters ripped across his back as he pivoted into a demolished stable.

The helicopter started its circling again—

—but the kerosene exploded with an earth-shattering roar. Blew the house apart directly under the helicopter, battering it with burning debris. A sickening whirlwind of chemical smoke and fire whipped across the lot, caught in the helicopter's rotor wash.

The pilot panicked. Jerked on the joystick. The helicopter banked sharply away from the explosion. Out of control.

Straight for the barn.

Kaiser dashed across the lot, opening up with the Ingram as he ran. Strafed the side of the helicopter. Hit the sniper, who fell screaming to his death, body crashing through the windshield of an enforcer's car. Blew the pilot's face off.

The helicopter plowed through the greenhouse and blasted through the connected barn, rotors shredding its walls like a giant buzz saw. Then it all erupted in a shower of wood splinters and metal. The ex-enforcer ducked behind the nearest car as a large portion of the barn came crashing down on the wreckage, belching fireballs and spraying debris. With burning wood chips came a light drizzle of snow.

Snow? In August? Kaiser was a miracle worker like that. It was snowing on the Murphy farm, only it had nothing to do with the weather. It was all cocaine.

Kaiser returned to his truck without a word. Discarded his Ingram. He never looked back. By the time he drove the truck out of the lot, the flaming barn had fully collapsed inward. The greenhouse had melted, scattered into the afternoon wind by the occasional explosion. The barn was no more. And Bill Murphy was cremated in his own home.

Chapter Twelve: Arms Race

The Donovan estate

Bacon sizzled in a skillet on the stove. Burnt. Unattended. The kitchen was empty. The gas was up way too high. Five minutes without attention—all the time in the world to catch fire.

As soon as he heard the shots echoing through the halls, and Candice's dying screams, Brad was quick to leave the kitchen. He knew who fired the shots. He didn't know why. Frankly, he didn't care. He just wanted to get as far away from the kitchen as possible. That was where he was last seen, after all.

He crept through the halls, holding the frying pan against his chest like a stuffed bear. It was more of a comfort to him than a weapon for self-defense. Light footsteps. Heart hammering against his ribcage. Every four steps, he froze, listening. Four steps. Froze. Four steps.

Noise. A brief, loud racket from behind a closed door.

Then a door four rooms down the hall opened. Brad scurried around the corner to the stairs. Glanced up the stairs at the third floor briefly. Peeked around the corner to see June's unmistakable slender figure rushing toward the opposite end of the hall. Barefoot. Red dress torn up, revealing considerably more skin than usual. Her left leg was totally exposed up to her waist. Shreds hanging off the dress swaying with her movements, flashing a portion of her bare buttocks in his direction.

Of course, Brad's eyes were glued to her ass the whole time. In his excitement, he shifted slightly. Something squeaked down the hall behind him. Brad looked down the opposite end of the hall.

The sound travelled.

June whirled, frantic. Fist clutching a severed shoulder strand to keep her dress from falling off. Bloodshot eyes. Brad was already out of sight.

Frightened. Cautionary. June gulped. Heaved a shuddering sigh. Stole one last glance over her shoulder. Turned her back and raced for the other set of stairs on the opposite side of the floor. Disappeared behind the oak railing.

Brad didn't know if the shots came from this floor or the third floor. He could avoid all confrontation and hide until Kaiser Corbane came around to clear the place out. Or he could look for a way out while everybody else would be (hopefully) too distracted by the shots to notice. Brad weighed his options. Went with the former. Dashed lightly down the hall. Entered the room he had just watched June exit.

The guest room.

Brad slowly entered the room. Stumbled over the broken glass in the carpet. Spotted a half-empty wine glass on the dresser half filled with a clear liquid. Picked it up. Sniffed it. "Hm." Took a sip, and realized it was some very fine-tasting champagne. "Mm!"

He stopped to stare at the blood stains in the carpet. Then listened to the sound of running water coming from the bathroom. Held his frying pan ready as he cautiously approached the bathroom door. Steam leaked through the crack in the door. The air got more humid the closer he got.

With a tentative hand, Brad pushed the bathroom door inward. Buffeted by a hot wave of steam and the smell of bleach. Foggy mirror. Bloody floor. No body to be found. The shower curtains weren't even drawn. No one was standing in the bathtub. Brad leaned forward. Peered into the tub. Found a yellow raincoat and a rusty ax lying in a jumbled pile, battered by water jets from the showerhead.

Brad coughed. This was getting to be a bit much. He needed another drink. Turned to leave. Stopped dead in his tracks. Found himself face to face with...

Jim couldn't believe it. Even while he stood by the bathtub, eyes focusing on the corpse sprawled in the tub, he couldn't believe it. He'd just emptied an entire clip into Candice Evergreen. A woman who could have been entirely innocent for all he knew. But she attacked Charley, didn't she? He said she was hiding the evidence. Why would he, a man succumbing to his wounds, lie about Candice is she wasn't trying to kill him? It didn't make any sense.

Although... here she was. Her blood on the broken glass walls. Smeared on the white tiles on the other side of the tub. Left eye was now an empty socket leaking red-and-white puss that oozed down her face to her jaw. Two more holes in her chest above her breasts.

Three in her stomach. Another in her thigh.

Jim stared at Candice's body until the shock wore off well enough for him to move. He trembled. Jittery. Shook it off.

He turned off the water and slowly backed out of the bathroom. Backed into the hall. Then broke into a solid run down the corridor. Shoes squeaking on the marble floor. Rounded the corner. Raced past the stairs. Passed the guest room—

Skidded to a stop at the sound of rushing water.

Jim glanced through the guest room doorway. Reloaded his pistol. Stepped inside just as Brad was coming out. Brad looked at him and stiffened.

Jim, pistol level with Brad's nose, asked, "What the fuck do you think you're doing in here, you little ponce?"

Brad opened his mouth but nothing came out. He shrugged. It was all he could get himself to do.

"Drop the frying pan."

Brad did as he was told. Tossed it on the footlocker. Cringed when it made a deafening noise.

Jim's eyes flickered to the bathroom door for a moment. "What were you doing in there?"

Brad still couldn't get himself to speak.

Impatient, Jim grabbed him by the collar and jerked him aside. Went into the bathroom. Looked down on the floor. Whirled around and asked, "Where the fuck is Charley?" When Brad didn't give an immediate answer, he shouted, "Where the fuck did you put Charley?!"

Brad threw his hands up. "T-tub!"

Jim looked into the tub. Saw the ax and the rain coat. Confused, he stormed out of the bathroom, keeping his gun fixed on Brad the entire time as he stepped out onto the balcony. Looked over the railing. The L-shaped object in the pool was still there. Jim turned to Brad. Said, "What the fuck is going on?" He squinted. "You... you did this, didn't you?"

"W-what?"

"You killed Twister and Charley, didn't you?"

"What?!" Brad exclaimed. "No! Ah didn't!"

"And you killed Nancy Corbane."

"No way!"

"I know the stink of bleach when I smell it. You're washing away the evidence and planting fake evidence. That ax in the pool...

what's the purpose of that compared to the one in the tub?" Jim scoffed and shook his head. "Or is my questioning the logic behind it the whole point? Well aren't you just the cheekiest little bastard."

"Ah swear, ah ain't killed anyone!"

"If it wasn't you, then it was June. And that bitch is nowhere to be found. Hell, she's probably dead, too. Ah, fuck it." Jim cocked the hammer of his pistol. "Maybe I should just do you both in and leave town. Let Kaiser interpret how the whole thing went."

"Whoa. Whoa. Whoa. Stop right there!" Brad said desperately. "Ah didn't... ah didn't kill anyone. Okay? A-ah just got here, and... this is all ah saw. What ye see is what ye get because it's all ah got, okay?! Ah saw June leave here! Ah'm too ossified ta kill anyone!"

"Maybe you are, maybe you aren't," Jim said. "I don't think that matters much anymore. Nancy Corbane was never here. Then somebody else went psycho and killed everyone else. Perhaps someone with an obsession with mystery board games...?" Jim raised an eyebrow. Smirked. The bastard had officially lost it.

"Wait a fuckin' minute," Brad said.

"As we speak, my brother's getting rid of the final piece of Nancy Corbane's involvement with this house. My house which, unfortunately, I'll have to burn down thanks to you lot. 'An electrical accident.' Hey, that means I'd have a nice insurance bonus for my trip."

"...So it were ye!" Brad shouted, pointing at him. "Ye did this! All this shit ta... ta collect insurance?!"

"Don't mistake my opportunism for responsibility," Jim said. "I didn't start this clusterfuck we've found ourselves in, but I'll be buggered if I'm not going to finish it. And what's wrong with devising an insurance scheme while I'm at it? At least my efforts won't be for free."

"Then what tha fuck were those shots?!"

"Jumping to conclusions. That was an accident."

"So ye are tha murderer!"

"I'm a murderer, but not, strictly speaking, the murderer."

"Did ye kill Nancy?"

"No."

"Oh, yeah? If ye didn't kill Nancy, then who did?!"

"Beats the bollocks out of me, mate," Jim said. "At this point, I don't particularly give a rat's arse who did it because you're all dead anyway. Sorry, Bradley. It's nothin' personal. It's just... insurance." Jim's eyes burned intensely.

Brad stared at him. Wide-eyed. Unsure of what to do. Then, suddenly, the words came pouring out of his mouth, slurred, "Run that by me again?"

Jim squinted. "What?"

"Ah don't get tha insurance part."

"I already explained to you. I'm not doing it again."

"Come on... ah'm gonna die anyway. Ah wanna have it clear in me brain for when ah ascend up the rainbow for me pot o' gold."

"Now you're just trying to buy time."

"For what?" Brad scoffed. "Ah'm fucked! Don't be such a bitch."

Jim sighed. "Alright, fine. I'm gonna make quick work of it: I kill whoever's left standing and then burn the house down. I collect the insurance. Kaiser can investigate all he wants. He won't find a damn thing about his wife that'll link her disappearance back to me or my brother. We get off scot-free with a great deal o' insurance cash with no worries an' no loose ends. Blah-blah-blah-blah-blah-blah."

"Great," Brad said. His face a mask of sober seriousness as he looked over Jim's shoulder. "Ya get all that, Charley?"

"What?!" Jim whirled around to find—

—an empty bathroom. "Shit!" Jim shouted as he turned back around to receive a frying pan in his face. The surprise attack sent him staggering against the dresser. The half-empty wine glass spilled over.

Brad swung the pan again. Smacked the gun right out of Jim's hand. Jim howled with rage and pain. Pounced on Brad. Their bodies locked, savagely throttling each other. Rolling over the footlocker. Crashing onto the balcony. Tumbling over the railing. Screaming. Plummeted into the deep end of the pool. Splash.

The freezing cold water was a good wakeup call. Brad was thrashing about. Frantically reaching for the edge of the pool.

Suddenly Jim burst out from behind him and latched on. Arm around Brad's neck. Pulled him back under. Breath, impossible. Panic took over as water filled Brad's lungs. He kicked the wall as he struggled against Jim's restraining arm. Slammed the back of his head into Jim's nose. The water turned red. Jim's arm slackened. Brad wrested free and clawed through the water to the edge. Hefted himself up with wobbling arms. Sucked in air. Relieved.

Jim's head resurfaced. Eyes clamped shut. Nose bleeding profusely. He clawed through the water, making violent splashes to the poolside.

Brad looked around the patio for something to fight with. All that looking around made him dizzy. He took a feeble step back and leaned on an outdoor table set. His eyes locked onto the folded parasol.

By the time Jim got out of the pool, Brad was wielding the parasol like a spear. The sight made Jim laugh, despite the burning pain shooting from his nose to his brain. "You don't scare me, Mary Poppins!"

"Whoop!" Brad yelled as the parasol flapped open right in Jim's face, sending him sprawling back into the pool.

"Oh! Bollocks!" Jim screamed just before falling in. His rage fuelled when Brad tossed the open parasol in after him. He started screaming obscenities and uttering threats that followed Brad across the patio, into the solarium.

As Brad ran, his mind screamed, Don't look back. Don't look back. Brad looked back.

Jim was scrambling out of the pool. A wild, angry beast. Uprooting pavement tiles as he crawled out. Rusty ax in his free hand, hacking the parasol to pieces. "You fucking wanker!"

A new wave of terror. Brad burst through the door and stumbled into the lobby. Wet feet slipped on marble. Cracked his face open on the floor. A white flash in his skull. Blurs. Shapes. Look at all the pretty colours.

No time to pass out. Brad was on his hands and knees, bolting for the stairs, haphazardly imbalanced as he ran.

A different solarium door came crashing down. Jim collapsed on top of it. Got up. Slipped on marble. Was more fortunate than Brad—landed on his shoulder. Groaned and practically skated on the ice-slick floor for the other set of stairs. By the time he reached the stairs on that side, Brad was making his way across the landing on the other staircase.

Both men, racing each other to the second floor.

For the dry, working gun on the guest room carpet.

Jim thundered up the stairs, stumbling here and there. His soaked clothing weighed him down. The ax in his hands weighed him down further—and threw off his balance.

Brad was having a lot more trouble getting up the stairs. His drunkenness had taken its toll. Everything spun like a blurry merry-go-round. Twirling lights. Feet pounding on the steps. Heavy, soaked suit. The suit was ruined.

Jim reached the top of the stairs. Raced down the hall. Ax swinging back and forth in his fists as if he were a hockey player in full charge for the puck. Slipped on marble. Fell flat on his face. "Shitting fuck!"

Brad wrapped his arms around the railing post and grunted as he pulled himself over the top step. "Oh, Jaysus, man..." Crawled around the post on his hands and knees, rising to a normal two-legged run down the hall...

...straight for Jim, who had just gotten to his feet. Brad didn't slow down. His vision was all over the place, but he knew where the door was. He was two doors down and closing. Jim was three doors away from the guest room and already in a fierce dash.

Brad charged straight for the man who was going to kill him. The door was ajar.

Jim was upon him. Bearing down on him like a behemoth. Ax raised high above his head. Swinging back down. Brad dived. Ax came down.

Brad tumbled into the guest room and kicked the door shut.

The ax snapped the knob out of the door.

Brad jumped up and locked the door with sweaty fingers while Jim cursed and swore on the other side. Muffled shouts. Fists banging on the door. The door wouldn't budge. Brad, soaked in sweat, heaved a relieved sigh. Safe.

A loud, sudden crack. The door split down the middle as the ax blade burst through it.

"Oh!" Brad screamed, taking a startled leap backwards. "Oh, shite!" He stepped on a chunk of glass. The bottom of the champagne bottle bit deep into his heel. Brad cried out and fell on his ass.

There, under the dresser where it'd been thrown, was the pistol. Brad snatched it up and aimed for the three doors that spun around in front of him. Shook his head. Vision became a little clearer, but not by much.

The door split apart. Jim kicked at the rest, shouting wildly.

Brad stood up. Levelled the pistol at the door. Fired three times through the splintery doorway.

Jim took one for certain. Threw him out of sight. The other two, Brad wasn't sure about.

Silence.

Brad stared at the doorway. Paralyzed with fear. Listening for a sound. Any sound. All while backing up toward the balcony in a limp. He considered jumping into the pool again.

The door had been almost completely destroyed. All that remained of it was the general structural outline and a few shards of wood stuck in the frame. The rest of it had been smashed to pieces, which were now strewn across the floor.

But Jim, gracious party host that he was, couldn't be found.

Chapter Thirteen: Rubber Tension

First things first.

Brad limped to the bathroom. Kept his wounded left heel off the floor. Leaving a blood trail in the carpet. He entered the bathroom and closed the door. Locked it just in case anyone else was still alive and didn't want him to be. He sat on the bathtub ledge and tended to his foot, which still had the champagne bottle's teeth biting around the ball of his foot. Brad grimaced as he pulled it out. "Ach!" He examined the round, bloody chunk of glass before wincing and throwing it into the trash bin beside the toilet. "Ah got ta get myself tha fuck outta here."

He turned around on the bathtub ledge and ran his bleeding foot under running water. Hissed as the cuts began to sting. Glanced at the ax and the yellow rain coat in the tub. He knew June was alive. He hadn't seen Charley. Twister, Candice, Jon, and Nancy were dead. He didn't know what the hell happened with Jeff and Al, and he wasn't quite sure if he hit Jim with a lethal shot.

And then there was the weird mixture of evidence. Two axes. A yellow raincoat. The Desert Eagle that killed Nancy Corbane. Maybe Jim was the murderer, and after he shot Nancy, he got everyone to clean up the evidence, instantly clearing him of suspicions for a while, which would buy him enough time to cut down the numbers in the group. Twister was hacked to pieces by an ax. Candice was fingered as the lead suspect, which may have led to Jim shooting her to death. Or maybe that was his way of telling everyone they were next so that he could make sure there was no one left alive to escape before he burned the house down. For insurance money...?

Brad shook his head slowly and started wiping his bleeding foot with a towel while keeping it under the faucet's running water. All of these possibilities and paradoxes were making his head spin. He looked at the ax and the raincoat again. "What am ah ta do?"

A jarring snap yanked him out of his thoughts. Brad turned to the door as an ax blade pierced it. Disappeared into the crack. Smashed through again.

Terror-struck once again, Brad lurched off the bathtub ledge, reaching for the gun on the counter. Missed it. Hit the floor and smacked into the cupboards, shaking the sink. The gun slipped over the edge of the shaken countertop and clattered to the floor. Brad grabbed it. Jumped to his feet. Winced and staggered awkwardly when he put weight on his bad foot. A piece of wood flew out of the door upon impact and hit the toilet. Brad aimed for the door.

The magazine fell out. It landed on the ceramic floor. Unbelievably, the clip snapped in half, spilling unused bullets and the spring across the tiles. "Oh! Shit." Brad squatted and quickly gathered up the bullets. Blurred vision making it next to impossible to determine where they actually were. Tried vainly—desperately— to shove them into the magazine port as—

—the ax head burst through the middle of the door. Snapped out a narrow chunk of wood that clattered inward. Brad screamed. Dropped the gun and the bullets. Reeled backwards against the far wall, terrified eyes on the door.

Jim. Crazed. Angry. A fucking psychotic. His true nature revealed. Pressed his face through the crack in the door. Bulging eyes fixed on his prey. "Heeeeeeere's Jimmy!"

"No!" Brad shrieked. "Git away! Fuck off!"

"No can do, ya Irish prick," Jim replied, still keeping his face pressed through the crack. "I'm gonna come in there, and I'm gonna chop you up into little fuckin' pieces! Twister's corpse ain't even gonna compare when I'm done with you, mate!" Jim's face retreated, replaced by his hand, which reached for the doorknob.

"Oh no ye don't, ya cocksuckin' British bastard!" Brad threw himself forward, slipping and sliding across the blood-soaked ceramic. Reached into the tub. Ax and the raincoat.

By then, Jim had the door wide open. Ax raised. Hollering wildly as he went for the killing blow.

Brad whirled and attacked Jim with the raincoat, throwing it over his assailant's head. Jim swung blind, but Brad was on him, driving his fist into Jim's face. Sent him flying into the corner. Slipped on the bloody floor. Crashed through the plastic toilet paper holder. Brad kicked him while he was down, landing his good heel into Jim's stomach twice before going back into the bathtub and taking out the other ax.

Jim struggled with the raincoat. A stream of profanity poured out of his mouth as he kicked and clawed at the coat, literally ripping through the rubber fabric with his fingernails and the ax blade.

Brad got the other ax. Swung for Jim's head.

Jim threw up his own ax and blocked Brad's killing blow with the wooden handle. He grabbed Brad's weapon and jerked on it, pulling him forward. Jim's foot lashed out. Caught Brad in the chest. Sent him sprawling into the bathtub.

With his prey momentarily disabled, Jim struggled some more with the raincoat, the slippery floor, and the extra ax—all while standing himself upright.

Brad fell out of the bathtub. Eyes lit up with terror when he saw his enemy coming to. Instantly broke into a run out the bathroom door.

Jim followed him into the guest room. Hurled an ax after him.

Brad dived through the splintered guestroom doorway. The ax spun over his head and smashed into a framed family picture on the other side of the hallway. Brad landed on the floor and rolled out of Jim's sight. He dashed down the hall, impaired greatly by his new limp, heel smearing blood on the floor during his getaway.

Jim roared from the guest room, "You can't hide forever!" His voice boomed through the halls. "I'll find ya! You cheeky, slippery bastard! I'll fuckin' find ya!"

Jim returned to the bathroom. Picked up his gun. Took his last clip from his back pocket and slapped it home. Jacked a new round into the chamber. Noticed a new, small ding on the slide. Snarled angrily, then shook his head and chuckled as he cocked the hammer. "Oh, for this, I might actually enjoy killing you, Brad."

He noticed the blood trail left in Brad's wake and grinned eagerly.

June heard the screaming from the third floor. She had been hiding in Jim's room. Having overturned everything, emptied all the drawers, and cleaned out the closet in her search for a weapon, June was surprised to find nothing but a gold letter opener to defend herself with. Given that this was Jim Donovan's room, she expected to find a pistol, at least.

Better than nothing, she thought.

June sniffed the air and discovered the faint, pungent odour of rotten eggs. She wrinkled her nose in disgust and opened her cigarette case to find, to her chagrin, that it was empty. "Goddamn it," she muttered as she tucked the case away in her purse.

She took her cell phone out of her purse. Didn't dial 9-1-1, but a private number reserved for emergencies. Usually she only called this number to get out of a different jam. A heist gone wrong. Persistent police heat. That sort of thing.

Instead of the man she was expecting on the other end, she got her service provider's automated voice messaging system: "You have insufficient funding to make this call."

"Are you serious?!" she exclaimed at the cell. When the voice message droned on, she folded her cell shut and shoved it back in her purse.

She went to the telephone on the dresser. Put the receiver to her ear and listened...

Absolutely nothing. Not even a dial tone.

The line was dead.

In a surge of frustration, all elegance and restraint forgotten, June snapped the cord and hurled the receiver at the wall, shattering it. "SHIT!" she screamed. "No cell phone service, no cigarettes, no phone line. Some party, Jim."

June sat at the foot of the bed. Composed herself. Felt her fingers over the knot she'd tied to keep the right shoulder string of her dress together. She stared at the door.

Then, letter opener in hand, she got up, crossed the room, opened the door, and stepped into the hallway. Entered the first door on her left.

Charley lay panting in Jim's office chair, staring at her. Still soaked in blood and laced with cuts and scratches.

Her elegant appearance and playful, seductive smile had instantly returned as soon as she stepped into the room. June held the letter opener at her side as she slowly approached her victim. "Now... where were we, Charley, darling?"

Chapter Fourteen: "Rosie Lee!"

Jim followed Brad's trail with his gun poised. He crossed the second floor. The blood trail led to the study in a jagged line, with a few diverging footprints into other rooms, probably vain attempts to throw him off. Not that it would have made a difference, since Jim had two other guests to find. He would have checked every door on his way to the study, anyway. He found nothing in the seven rooms leading up the hall to the study.

When he entered the study, the trail had suddenly gone cold. A single red footprint on the study floor, and that was it. There was no more sign of Brad. Just like in all the other rooms.

Frustrated, Jim looked around the room. Checked under the desk. Behind the armchair. Turned and looked over at the liquor cabinet.

Brad had himself squeezed behind it, his back flat against the wall. Hand tightly pressed over his mouth and nose to mask his breathing.

Jim approached the liquor cabinet. Went into the hidden compartment at the bottom and took out a crystal bottle of rum. He didn't bother with a glass as he chugged down a third of the bottle before shattering it against the nearest wall.

Brad flinched at the sharp noise. Ever so slightly. The glasses in the cabinet clinked.

Jim looked at the cabinet. He thought he noticed movement in the corner of his eye. He stared at the cabinet. Squinted.

Brad held his breath.

Jim shrugged and belched.

And, with that, he left the study.

Hidden in the study. Behind the liquor cabinet.

From there, Brad was still shaken from the close call he'd just had. He smelled a foul mixture of something burning and rotten eggs. At that moment, he remembered that he'd left the stove on. That bacon had to have been burnt to crispy pieces by now. He knew he had to shut off the gas before Jim started shooting again.

"Aw, shit," he said to himself as he squeezed out of his hiding place. Tiptoed to the closed door. Opened it a crack. Searched around the balcony that overlooked the foyer.

All clear.

He stepped out. Jogged across the hall toward the staircase to the foyer. Stopped when he heard a noise from the top of the third floor stairs. He looked up to see an avalanche of little smiley face ornaments coming down from the third floor. Like hundreds of rubber balls, they bounced and sprang off the steps. Pitter-patter-pitter-patter.

Brad stiffened as he watched these ornaments flood the hall around him. Surrounding him like a yellow sea of flowers. Then they all looked up at him with black dot eyes and laughed. Squeaky, evil cackles filled his ears. A haunting chorus that mocked his desperation. Brad kicked at them, only for more of them to fill whatever spaces he'd made in doing so. Laughing. Deafening.

"Shut tha fuck up!" Brad screamed. He ran with a fierce limp toward the next door. Burst through it. Found himself in a bland white hallway. It was like one of those choking halls with shiny marble floors and fluorescent lights hanging from the ceiling. Always on, even with the sun shining through big windows that ran down the hall on one side.

What tha hell?

Brad raced down the hall, which stretched on and on. As he passed every window, the scenery changed. Children laughing on a playground. A gunfight in the street between cops and robbers. A family watching TV in a dark room. A wedding recital.

And the voices. Voices from the past. Voices from people he thought he'd never see or hear again.

"Son, I'm gonna teach you how to rob banks..."

"...suspended from school, liquor found in his backpack..."

"That orange shirt looks terrible on you."

"Blow me."

"Fucking Irish prick!"

Down he went. The voices got louder. Deafening. His footsteps, more hollow. The walls were closing in on him. Faces smeared over them. Screaming projections. His uncle's contagious laughter ringing through the hall, following him.

"Mum? Mum?"

A concussive *bang*. The walls now splattered red with blood. Crimson lightning strobed the windows.

"MUM!"

"Soon, son, you'll be a motherless plonker just like me."

A women's shrill scream.

"Filthy thieving cunts!"

Finally, a door appeared at the end of the tunnel. Brad raced toward it. A train's horn blared behind him, getting closer... closer...

He scrambled through the doorway. All went quiet.

Twister Chay stood with his back facing him.

Jim appeared beside Brad with the ax in his hands, dressed in the yellow raincoat. Brad yelped with surprise and leaped back.

Jim called out to Twister. Friendly. Playful. "Oi, mate!"

Twister turned.

Jim roared savagely. All friendliness gone. Raised the ax.

Twister's face, now distorted with terror.

The ax split his face in two. June pulled the ax out and hacked savagely at Twister's body. Jim was nowhere to be found.

Candice swung the ax down on Twister. Split his chest open. Blood sprayed. Severed fingers flew around. Brad looked on in horror as a dozen skeletons laughed raucously around the ballroom table, having a tea party of their own. The Grim Reaper himself sat at the head, sipping from a teacup between amused chuckles at the sight.

Brad turned toward the scene of the killing again. Now Jon, still with a tunnel burned through his face, had the ax. He severed Twister's right arm with it.

Brad looked at the tea party skeletons as they greedily wolfed down scones and biscuits, laughing heartily at the display.

Charley had the ax now. He pulverized Twister's still-beating heart. Then Twister's eyes opened wide, and even he started laughing. "Oh, the pain! You're so... twisted!"

The tea party skeletons banged the table with their fists and guffawed. The table shook so much that teacups and desserts started rolling onto the floor.

Brad ran for the nearest exit. Slipped on something. Fell forward, then quickly scrambled to his feet. Looked down to see the rusty ax in his hands. He was dressed in the bloodied raincoat, all neatly buttoned up. Brad threw the ax away and tore the raincoat off. "Jaysus! Jaysus!"

Brad threw another door open. Found himself in a circus where the audience members and the performers had giant smiley face ornaments as heads. It was a full house. On the stage in the middle of the tent, giant puppets resembling the tea partygoers and Kaiser Corbane pranced around on strings. A model helicopter came crashing down, accompanied by someone imitating sound effects on speakers.

"Suddenly, Kaiser Corbane came outta nowhere! They thought they were safe!" the narrator cackled as the Kaiser puppet brought up a chainsaw and slaughtered all ten partygoers. The puppets came apart in a wild blood spray. Wooden limbs flew in all directions as the narrator shouted, "THEY WERE WRONG!"

The audience exploded into a wild, cackling uproar. Deafening. Crazy.

The entire circus tent shook violently. The ear-splitting sound of a toilet flushing. Then everything—the stage, the audience, the tent—crumbled away into a downward spiral. Brad, caught in the current, screamed in terror as a massive black hole swallowed him along with everything else.

Darkness.

Then a black-and-white projection screen: 3... 2... 1...

Brad found himself standing in a dark room, staring at a tarp with the image superimposed on it. He whirled around to see the old projector. Reels spinning. Flickering. He turned back to the screen as the image of Jesus nailed to the cross appeared. Jesus was smiling at Brad, saying, "I died for your sins. Kaiser's gonna kill you for yours."

Brad broke down in tears. He fell on his knees and wailed at the image projection, "Oh, Jaysus, make it stop! Ah'll never drink again!"

"Stop grovelling! You're so pathetic! So pathetic, it makes me laugh!" And, with that, Jesus started laughing wildly.

A Roman stepped into the frame and snarled, "Quiet you!" Stabbed his ribs with a spear.

Jesus continued to laugh. "My sides!"

The picture burned out. Melted away.

The floor gave out under Brad's feet. Gave way. Brad shrieked, arms flailing, as he plummeted through darkness. His deceased uncle chanting like an omnipresent voice, "Rosie Lee! Rosie Lee!"

"Rosie Lee! Rosie Lee! Rosie Lee!"

Jim stood in the doorway of the study, gaping at the sight of Brad throwing himself around the room, screaming and babbling as if he'd just completely lost it. Knocking over the chair. Tearing down the curtains.

Jim shouted at him. "Hey! Hey!"

Brad didn't respond. Instead, he dived straight into the liquor cabinet with a deafening crash. He hit the floor. The smashed cabinet fell on top of him, spilling liquor and glass across the study floor.

"Oi!" Jim roared angrily, stomping into the study with his pistol aimed at Brad. "Stop fuckin' my place up! Goddamn arseholed bastard! Look at this mess! Look at it!"

Brad coughed and sputtered. He shifted slightly, pinned to the floor by the cabinet. He looked up at Jim, blinking several times. "What d'ye care? Ye're gonna burn it down anyway."

"True enough." Jim pointed his pistol at him. "Cheerio."

White flash. Thunder crackled.

He fell into a swirling abyss. Wind whistling. Ground rising up to meet him—

Then Brad's head lurched off the pillow. He screamed at the top of his lungs, thrashing around in sanitized sheets. "JAYSUS! JAYSUS! OH SHITE! JAYSUS! SHITE!"

A trio of nurses swarmed around him, doing their best to console him. Screams of terror were all he was capable of. He kicked a silver tray out of the blonde nurse's hands. Syringes, bottles, and a glass of water shattered against the far wall. The nurses protested as they restrained him. The blonde and the brunette pinned his limbs to the bed while the redhead sedated him.

In seconds, Brad's frantic behaviour had been drained from his system.

"It was just a bad dream," the blonde said soothingly as she dabbed his sweaty forehead with a cool, damp cloth. "Shh... there, there."

Brad panted heavily as he looked around the hospital room. He looked at the heartbeat monitor, then the strengthened windows overlooking the modest skyline of downtown Cherry Springs. Then he looked at the room exit on the other side. Lighting wasn't like that of a hospital. The room was tinged sea blue. Surreal. Dreamlike. Calming.

"Where am ah?" he asked.

"You're in a hospital," the redhead answered.

Brad felt his head and realized it was swathed in gauze. "What tha hell's on my head?"

"You were shot," the brunette said. "We treated your wounds."

"What about the estate?" he asked. "The house? Nancy? Jim... what happened to Jim?!"

"Calm yourself," the brunette said, laying a gentle hand on his shoulder. "We'll take good care of you."

"What about the estate? What happened to the party?" he asked.

The blonde injected him with another sedative. "Shh."

"Just a bad dream," the redhead said.

"Only a dream," Brad gasped. "It was all... a dream?"

"It's all in your head." The redhead put a playful finger to his lips.

Then, suddenly, the trio vanished without a trace. The sea blue tinge switched dramatically to blood red.

Despite the sedatives, Brad started to panic. The deep red tinge seemed like a drop into hell. He looked around the room. Froze up when he saw the blonde's corpse splayed out in the doorway with a scalpel in her forehead. "Jaysus!" he exclaimed as he scrambled out of bed.

The overhead lights buzzed and flickered ominously. The red tinge was everywhere. So were the bodies. Standing in the doorway, Brad surveyed the halls in horror. Heart pounding against his ribcage like a jackhammer. Patients and hospital staff littered the halls, butchered like pigs in a slaughterhouse. Some were strung up on hooks, suspended from the ceiling. Others were draped through partition walls. On the other side of the hall, a sea of flames raged. Out of control. Consuming every corpse in its path as it spread through the hospital like a highly contagious disease that could be seen by the naked eye.

A dark figure emerged from the maternity ward, engulfed in fire. A demon. The double doors parted open like the gates of hell. Screaming newborns wailed behind him.

Kaiser Corbane. Extremely pissed off. Eyes blazing. Armed to the teeth. The Ingram in one hand and the big fucking cannon in the other. He pointed both at Brad.

Brad screamed and retreated to his room. Bullets blew out the partition window and ripped through the blinds. Punched holes through the bed. Weakened the wall-to-ceiling windows on the other side of the room. Crystallized them. Brad dived behind his bed to escape the never-ending volley. Feathers exploded from the pillow. Sparks flew as the heart monitor blew apart.

Brad threw himself out the window. Sailed through space in a shower of glass. Plummeted into flaming pits. The buildings of Cherry Springs shattered and poured into the hellish void in an avalanche. Everything fell away like sand. Brad's screaming, drowned out by the roar of destruction. The hospital pancaked behind him and started to slide over his head. Crashing down... bearing down...

Resounding crash as the liquor cabinet pinned him to the floor. For real this time. Brad looked around the study. There was no sign of Jim. No bullet casing. No blood from getting shot. Only a throbbing headache.

Confusion took hold. Followed by panic and fear. Cold sweat. Trembling hands. Brad clawed at the carpet as he struggled with the cabinet that rested on his legs. "Ah gotta get me tha fuck outta here!"

Chapter Fifteen: Sympathy for the Maid

Jim stepped into his office. Gun ready. Eyes fixed on Charley, who was slumped in his chair behind the desk. Lifeless.

Now he was sure who the real killer was.

Leaving the office, Jim called out, "June. Come out, ya fuckin' slapper. The jig is up." He turned and opened his bedroom door. He was appalled to find it in such a mess. "You'll be cleanin' that up before I put one in ya!" he shouted angrily. "What kinda guest puts their host's room in fuckin' shambles like that?"

He moved to the bathroom. Swiped the shower curtains to look into the tub. Searched the cupboards under the sink. Then moved on when he found it empty.

June hid in the library. It was one of the biggest rooms in the house, excluding the foyer and the ballroom. Bookshelves touched the ceiling—seven in the middle of the room, lined up perfectly; eight standing against the walls, parted by windows that let the orange light of the sunset into the room.

The door opened. The hinges creaked.

June dropped to a squat in the third row. She peered through the lower shelves to see Jim step inside, and watched him move toward the windows. June scurried down the aisle in the opposite direction that her pursuer was travelling and ducked behind the side of the shelf. Standing stiff as a log, June kept her back pressed against the shelf as Jim's shadow crept across the sunlit spots on the floor. First on her left. It disappeared into the shadow of the shelf she stood behind. Then, finally, his shadow reappeared on her right side. He moved on, none the wiser.

She had a clear view of the door. Perfect chance.

June slipped out of her high heels. Barefoot, she bolted for the exit, quiet as a mouse. She grabbed the door handle in a sweaty fist. Turned it slowly, stealing a cautionary glance at the shelves for any sign of her pursuer.

The door opened. The hinges creaked.

The sound cut through the still air. June inhaled sharply. Heart leaped in her throat. She knew Jim heard, because the faint pattern of his footsteps had suddenly stopped.

"Oi! Slapper!" he shouted from the fifth row.

June scrambled out of the library. Pulled the door shut behind her. Jim had already reached the door and smashed through it.

The door splintered. The hinges burst.

Frantic, Jim looked around. Too late. Somehow June had managed to disappear. "I will find you, bitch!" he roared.

Then... a sudden racket on the lower floor caught his attention. Was it her? Did she slip up or knock something over during her escape?

No. It was the liquor cabinet falling on Brad, fresh out of the weirdest trip he'd ever had since high school. After some struggling, Brad managed to crawl out from under the cabinet. Then he staggered drunkenly to the door. Dizzy as hell. Knocking over papers and desktop items in the process as he tried to walk straight in a spinning carousel room.

When he finally reached the door, he quickly threw it open and collapsed in the hall. He rushed toward the stairs. Reached the top. Grabbed the railing. Started down—

"Ah-ah!"

Froze. Brad turned his head slowly and found himself staring down Jim's M1911 pistol. "Fuck."

"Yeah, 'fuck' is right, you Irish prick," Jim said. "You're more trouble than an idiot drunk like you is worth." He gestured for Brad to get back up the stairs. Brad obeyed, stopping at the top step, hands up.

"Ah dinna do anythin' to deserve this treatment," Brad said, voice shaking. "Ya oughtta treat ye guests with more respect."

"Yeah, this late in the game, that's not gonna work, mate," Jim said.

"Ye dinna understand!" Brad exclaimed. "Tha oven! Makin' rashers, I was. It's...!" He found his voice trailing off when June stumbled into view, coming down the stairs from the third floor and turning into the hallway. As soon as Brad saw her approaching, he threw up an accusing finger and shouted, "Ah knew it! It was her all along! All calm an' casual amidst the scene o' the crime. Ya played us all for fools. Played us against each other like ye own personal fuckin' lab rats! Ya like ta play with people's minds. Ya said it yeself. It was ya all along, wasn't it? It was ya! The fuckin' plot!

It culminates!"

Jim turned and stared at her, as if the revelation's possibility had just donned on him.

"Ya see?!" Brad said to Jim. "She knew this shit would happen! Ya volatile, stupid fuck! She anticipated ye every move before ya even shot Candice!"

Jim looked at him with raised eyebrows. "But... Candice was an accident. She... Charley told me she was the murderer!"

"It weren't Candice," Brad said, eyes lighting up. "This whole time, it were June! Ye bitch, playin' our strings like that! What've ye got ta say for yeself?!"

June stopped walking. Stood staring at them like a deer caught in the headlights. She said, "Wrong."

Fell forward. Dead. Letter opener sticking out of her back.

Revealing Charley a few paces behind her with a bread knife in his left hand. Alarmed, Jim pointed his gun at Charley. Brad exclaimed, "Holy fuckin' shit! It was him! It was Charley all along!"

Charley's wide eyes seemed fixed on something behind them. He asked, "Am I the only one who sees that elephant?"

Jim furrowed his brows. "What fucking elephant?"

Brad kept shouting, "He did it! He's tha murderer!"

"Yes... I did what I had to," Charley said. The regret was clear in his voice. "I couldn't take another minute here. I didn't want to be fingered as the murderer, but... I didn't want to wait for that damn Kaiser Corbane to show up just so he could kill us all. I wanted to live. I was... I am... willing to do anything to survive. I'm not going to die because of my friend's stupidity. To hell with that."

Jim and Brad exchanged looks. Then Jim said, "What the bloody hell are you talking about? Are you saying you... didn't kill Nancy Corbane?"

"Of course not! For the few hours that I'd known her, she was like a sister-in-law to me, despite the fact that Jon and I weren't related... but we were like brothers!"

"And you sent me to kill Candice," Jim hissed with disgust. "Like your fuckin' hitman."

"As much as I'd hate to admit it, yes, I used you to my own—" Charley suddenly collapsed. Gargled. Choked. Wheezed, "Goddamn... it." Head hit the floor. Knife clattering on the marble tile. Hands clutching his stomach. Trembling violently.

Jim shook his head, smirking triumphantly. "Forgive me if this is a bit of a stretch, but... I bet our friend June here was thinkin' the same thing. She must've poisoned the champagne. In a way, she killed you before you killed her. Heh. Hell hath no fury like a woman scorned." Jim paused. Turned to Brad. "With all that alcohol you've been drinking, didn't you drink champagne, too?"

Brad chuckled. "Nah."

Then he keeled over. Toppled down the stairs. Crashed at the bottom on the foyer floor. A twisted heap. Dead.

Jim looked at the three bodies that he now stood over. Shrugged, unsure of what else to do. "Crikey. I won. I lived! I survived the fuckin' tea party affair!"

Charley moaned in agony. "Help..."

Jim turned. Looked down on him in disgust. Raised his .45. "Oh, belt the fuck up."

Pulled the trigger.

Pause. By this time, the bacon had been burning on the stove for over thirty minutes. Gas, unattended.

Play.

BOOM!

The flames only took a moment to fill the place. Then the Donovan Estate concussively blew apart. Three storeys of brick and shingles went up in a fireball. Night became day. Above the deafening cacophony was the ear-splitting tinkle of shattering glass. A wall of flame, erected like the walls of Jericho. A hail of shrapnel sprayed across the front lawn, shredding the well looked-after grass. Debris crashed down in sections.

In seconds, the house was gone. Flattened. All that remained was a vast patch of blazing shit. Smoke filled the sky. Blotched out the stars. Nothing left worth salvaging.

The maid had her work cut out for her.

Chapter Sixteen: Sweet Dreams Down the Road

Jeff and Al

A roadside diner called Halley's Diner. The jukebox played old classics all day, every day. The bright colours were both cool and welcoming.

Al and Jeff were seated in a pink vinyl booth, reading the menus whilst waiting for the waitress to bring their drinks around.

"Just doesn't seem right," Jeff said from behind the pages of his menu.

Al set his menu flat on the table and asked, "What doesn't, mate?"

Jeff put his menu down. "This whole fucking situation. This whole fucking situation doesn't seem right."

"Yeah?"

"Yeah, I mean, we're getting rid of a filing cabinet that's covered in blood."

"Yeah? So?"

"What if your brother did it?"

"Again with the 'your brother is the killer' bollocks," Al said, agitation flaring. "It's getting on my nerves."

"Did you already go senile or something?" Jeff exclaimed, not quite loud enough to disturb any other patrons. "He made us clean up the crime scene and then killed the guy she was fucking, for fuck's sake," Jeff said. "That makes so much sense, it just might be true."

"Or it might not be true."

"You're just saying that because you're his brother."

"No, I'm saying that because my brother's more honest in that regard. If he were gonna kill us, or get rid of the evidence, he would've been a lot more straightforward. We wouldn't even be here right now. He would've just taken those two guns and blasted us all to guano."

"Maybe it's all a ruse or some shit."

"Now you're just grasping at fuckin' straws." Al leaned back when the redheaded waitress arrived with their milkshakes. He looked at her and asked, "What's your name, sweetheart?"

The young waitress pointed at the gold nametag on her ample chest. "Name's Jenny," she said.

"Jenny, huh," Al said. "How old are you?"

"Too young for you, sir," she said. "Nineteen."

Al looked at Jeff. "Thought that was legal?"

Jeff stared at him. "You're like fifty. It might be legal, but it's fucking disgusting."

"I'm not fifty, I'm thirty-four, you wanker." Al shrugged. Looked at Jenny again. "Ah well. Sorry if I bothered you, miss. Didn't quite mean it to be rude."

Jenny shrugged. "I get weirder all the time. No big deal. So... have you guys come up with what you wanna eat, yet?"

"Uh yeah, lessee," Jeff said as he took a quick look through the menu. "Chili cheese burger with fries."

Jenny wrote it on her notepad, then looked at Al. "You?"

"Same," he said.

"Two chili cheese burgers with fries," she said as she wrote 'Piss on the second order' in the margin. With a smile, she said, "Comin' right up." As she walked away, her expression darkened to a frown. She muttered, "Fucking pervert."

When the waitress was out of earshot, Jeff asked Al, "What the hell was that?"

"What?" Al asked.

"That. Don't play the innocent card, you assholish Brit shithead."

"All I did was ask for her name and her age."

Loud squeaking stopped their conversation dead as their curiosity piqued. Before either man could look, a nineteen-year-old boy rolled backwards into view. Stopped his wheelchair beside their booth. Glared at them with cold blue eyes behind aviator sunglasses. The thing that got their attention first was the teenager's unusually messy cobalt blue hair.

For a quiet minute, the two men had a staring competition with the boy in the wheelchair.

Then, coolly, the boy drew a Smith & Wesson Model 500 revolver from the inner breast pocket of his jacket and pointed it at Al. Both men went stiff as statues as the boy said calmly, "Talk to my girl like that again... and I'll kill ya."

And, with that, his electric wheelchair continued to squeak backwards toward the counter, haunting eyes never losing sight of

Al. None of the other patrons in the diner seemed to notice.

Al and Jeff exchanged looks. Jeff asked, "What the fuck was that?"

"I don't know," Al said as he looked at the boy again. "But I didn't like it."

Across the diner, the boy was still staring at him. At one point, Jenny approached him with their orders on a tray, said something to him, then kissed his cheek and moved on to their table.

"Here you go," she said cheerfully as she set Al and Jeff's orders down in front of them.

"Uh, can I ask you a question?" Al asked her, still watching the wheelchair guy—who was still staring at him.

"You just asked a question, sir," she said matter-of-factly.

Ignoring her comment, Al asked, "What's his problem?"

Without turning around to see whom Al was referring to, Jenny said, "That's just Damian. He's not really a people person."

"I noticed," Al said, still shaken. "Why's he staring at me?"

"Because you talked to me for like, more than two seconds, probably."

"Jealous friend of yours?" Jeff asked.

"Jealous boyfriend." Jenny smiled. "He's a psychopath, but I love him anyway."

Al looked past Jenny again. Damian was still staring at him like a cat targeting a mouse. Nervous, Al asked, "Can we get our meals on the go and have our cheques now, please?"

"Sure thing," she said. Then she left. Started around the counter to the register. Tousled Damian's hair along the way as if he was her pet cat. Damian, in the meantime, was still glaring at Al.

"Jesus Christ, there was something wrong with that shit," Al said as they crossed the parking lot to their van. They each had their respective meals in takeout boxes. Al glanced over his shoulder at the glass walls that boxed in the dining area of the diner. Inside, Damian was still staring at him, having parked his wheelchair next to the exit.

Al turned back around and shuddered.

Jeff looked back and laughed. "Never try to paint another man's fence."

"Yeah, yeah," Al said as he climbed into the driver seat.

They peeled out of the parking lot. Back on the road. It didn't take long for Jeff to start with his 'suggestions' again.

"We should just keep going," Jeff said.

"Keep going? What?"

"I mean we should skip town. Leave this whole thing behind us while we've got the chance."

"I ain't leavin' my brother back there, mate."

"We should."

"No, we really shouldn't. We're just gonna take this cabinet and bury it somewhere."

"Where?"

Al shrugged. "I don't know."

"Call him and ask him... if he hasn't killed everyone yet."

"Oh, belt up," Al said as he took out his cell phone and hit speed dial 4.

After a short ring, Jim answered. "Hello?"

"Evenin', bro," Al said. "How far out should I drive?"

"As far as you can manage. I don't want that filing cabinet to be found for at least ten years."

"Goddamn it. Any exact ideas?"

"Where are you?"

"Approaching the suspension bridge." Al saw Jeff reach for the stereo and slapped his hand until it recoiled. "I might be, uh... maybe five kilometres away from the house."

"Only five? You've been driving for over an hour and you only covered a five-kilometre distance?"

"We stopped to get something to eat."

"...You stopped at a restaurant... in a public place... with a bloody filing cabinet in the back of your van?"

"Yeah. Is there a problem?" Al glared at Jeff as he reached for the stereo again. He smacked his passenger's shoulder and sharply pointed at his phone.

"Yes, there's a fucking problem, you blithering idiot!" Jim exclaimed from the other side. "We have a very limited amount of time before Kaiser Corbane gets to my house!"

"So what? We've got the last of the evidence in the back."

"If he notices that there's a filing cabinet missing, he'll get suspicious, Al. And I don't want Kaiser Corbane to feel any more suspicious than he'll already be when he comes in askin' for his wife. Before you get back, I want you to make a quick pit stop at a department store and pick up an exact replica of the cabinet you buried.   I want everything perfect.   Aside from the potential murderer lurking in my estate, you're the final loose end. Or rather, that cabinet is, and I want you to tie it up."

"Alright, alright. It'll be—hey!" he shouted when Jeff touched the power button on the stereo. "Don't touch that."

Something wrong?" Jim asked.

"It's just Jeff fucking with my stereo." Al grabbed Jeff's wrist. "Sod off, you prick!"

Jeff shot back, "You sod off, you British bastard!"

"I'll kick you out of this fucking car, mate!"

With Al getting distracted, there was no one to watch the road.

"Bullshit, I've got my seatbelt on," Jeff said.

"What the fuck's your problem?"

"He's a murderer. Why should we listen to murderers?" Jeff stabbed the power button. Metallica blasted through the speakers.

"You fucking son of a bitch," Al shouted as he switched the stereo off.

"He's a goddamn murderer, don't believe his lies," Jeff exclaimed as he opened his takeout box and hurled it into the ceiling, spraying fries and burger bits everywhere.

"OH!" Al screamed as he shielded himself from the food. "Mary, mother of shit!"

Everything went to an abrupt stop when the van collided with a pickup in the wrong lane. A concussive explosion of metal and shattered glass as Jeff traded places with the pickup driver through obliterated windshields. Al's face smashed off the steering wheel right before the airbag blew up in his face, breaking his neck. The pickup driver hurtled between the van's front seats and plowed into the filing cabinet. The van's rear doors flew apart as the pickup driver and the filing cabinet crashed out onto the road. Tumbled down the lane. Metal flying. Cabinet cart-wheeling. Pickup driver sprawled out on the asphalt. Al sandwiched between the seat and the airbag. Jeff slumped over the dashboard and cup holders in the pickup truck, feet propped on the crumpled hood. Smoke rose up from the impact point where the two engines tried to swallow each other.

Behind the van, next to the filing cabinet that marked the final piece of evidence to his wife's murder, Kaiser Corbane stared lifelessly at the afternoon sky.

An hour later, Damian and Jenny arrived on a motorcycle. Jenny drove up to the driver side window and looked at Al's shattered face, indifferent to the horrific aftermath of the crash. Damian's wheelchair had been tied to the back of motorcycle, as if it were being towed, with Damian strapped into it. He observed the scene with a satisfied smirk.

Damian said, "Sweet dreams, motherfuckers," right before Jenny roared down the highway with him sitting in the back, smiling at the crash site until the gap between them was too large for him to maintain interest.

Chapter Seventeen: I Now Denounce You, Husband and Wife

Corbane residence

The office phone rang first thing in the morning. Kaiser Corbane was still sleeping soundly in his bedroom. Alone. Muscles tense even during the most pleasant of dreams. Sunlight just now peeking over the horizon. Thin golden rays slicing through the blinds. The still air carried the phone's racket across the house.

The phone went to voicemail: "Mr. Corbane, it's your ever-so-cheerful private eye speaking." A light smoker's cough rasped through the machine before he continued, "Unfortunately, I've got nothing but bad news to spoil this pleasant Sunday morning. I think it's safe to say that your suspicions of your wife were justified. I, uh... I tailed her for a few days, like you requested, and during the third day, she went to a house owned by a guy named Jon Whitby. Likely related to the local drug dealer, Bill Whitby. As I recall from past records, you used to work for him. I guess that complicates things further.

"Anyway, she went to his house... and she slept with him for a good portion of the afternoon. Again, I'm so sorry about being the bearer of bad news. Trust me, this is my least favourite part of the job. I have the photographs. I don't think you'd want to see them, but if you do, then... well... stop by my office, then. My secretary will give them to you once you drop your name. Goodbye."

The tea party at the Donovan estate

The phone's shrill ringing cut across the ballroom from the kitchen. Jim got up and said, "I'll get that. You guys make yourselves comfortable."

When Jim left, Brad asked Al, "Where's tha bog?"

"Which one?"

"Tha most durable," Brad said. "Feelin' tha runs comin' on."

"Upstairs. Second floor. Fifth door from the staircase on your right."

Brad stared at him. "Which staircase?"

With a sigh, Al got up, rounded the table, and helped Brad out of his chair. "Come on, you sod. I'll bring ya to it."

Brad reached out at the last second and took his wine bottle with him.

As Brad and Al left the ballroom, June stood up and headed for the foyer. "If anyone needs me, I'll be getting a fresh pack of smokes from my car."

Twister and Charley left their seats, taking their dessert plates and teacups with them. "We'll be in the library," Twister said before saying to Charley, "I'm kind of envious of Jim's collection."

"So am I," Charley replied. "I wouldn't mind seeing it again. Maybe this time I can give it a more thorough look. There were some interesting-looking books that I didn't get the chance to look at."

"Why's that?" Charley asked.

"We had a busy schedule that day. Two jobs in a single day. It's really strenuous. Jim can be a slave driver when he wants to be."

As their voices faded down the hall and up the stairs, out of sight, Candice found herself alone with Jon and Nancy. With a knowing snicker, she got up and said, "I'll leave you two lovebirds alone."

Nancy sputtered, "It's not like that, you silly girl!"

Jon was flustered, but he said nothing.

"Bye, now," Candice sang. She did a little wave as she pranced out of the ballroom.

Uneasiness fell between the two guests. They locked eyes, then looked away just as quickly. Nancy giggled and drew a lock of hair behind her ear.

Jon decided to be the conversation-starter. "How have you been doing for yourself?" he asked.

"Oh, I've been doing alright. I haven't done much since that birthday party thing I told you about."

"The jewel thing with Garden?"

She nodded. "Yeah. Would you believe it, she broke my hand in three places."

"How's it coming along?"

"It's just about healed, but it still hurts sometimes." She glanced at her hand. She was wearing green gloves that went up to her elbows. "It's been quiet while I've waited for this hand to heal."

"Can I see it?"

She looked at him. A twinkle in her eye. A smile on her face.

"And what could you do about it?"

Jon returned the smile and shrugged. "Nothing, really. I just want to see how it looks."

Still smiling, Nancy held her hand across the table. allowing Jon to take it. Jon slid the glove off her hand and held her bare hand firmly in both of his. He felt over the red lines, the little scars where the stitches once were, with the tenderness of a veterinarian on an injured kitten. Not even the scars could ruin her soft skin.

"They've healed nicely," he said. "The scars."

"I know I'd be asking too much for them to completely disappear. But... that's life. We can't always get what we want. That's just not how life works. I honest to God wish it did, but... it doesn't."

Jon got the hint. His gaze fell to the table, discouraged. Released her hand and fidgeted his own hands around his dessert plate. "I know it would never plausibly work out between us. Because of him."

Nancy's smile had completely vanished. She took his hand back and grasped it firmly. "What if it could work out? Without him? Without Kaiser?"

Jon looked at her. Eyebrows high. To hear her say this was both a shocking nightmare and a wonderful surprise. "But... but how?"

"I can get us out of here. We can—"

The cell phone. A flowery ringtone.

With a sigh, Nancy released Jon's hand and rummaged through her purse. Took out the cell. Looked at the caller ID. She stood out of her chair and said to Jon, "Can you wait outside of the room, please? I need to take this..."

Jon stared at her, hesitant.

"It's my husband," she added.

Jon nodded slowly. Got up. Left the ballroom through the foyer entrance.

The Corbane residence

Kaiser heard the message an hour later. Fuelled with rage, he called up his wife. Nancy Corbane answered the phone with a sweet, loving, "Yes, husband?"

"Don't," he growled.

"What's the matter?" she asked.

"I know about you and that fucking Whitby bastard."

Nancy said nothing. She was too shocked to respond.

"What I want to know is... why?"

Nancy still didn't respond.

Impatient, Kaiser said, "You don't want to talk, huh? Well that's just fine by me. I'll find out when I get there."

"You're still coming here...?"

"Damn right I am, and when I get there, I'm gonna fucking kill you. But first, I'm gonna kill Jon right in front of you. And then I'm going to kill whoever else knew about you whoring around with a drug dealer's brother, and forgot to mention it to me. Even if it's every single one of those lowlifes attending that party."

"Please, it's not—"

"Bullshit, bitch!" Kaiser shouted. Then his voice shrank to a menacing snarl, "I'll be up there in a few hours. That should be more than enough time for you to pray to your god and say goodbye to your social groups. And don't bother trying to run with your new lover. There will be no place you can run where I won't catch up to you. There will be no place for you to hide where I can't find you. There won't even be a spot for you to climb up to without me already waiting for you at the top. You're fucked, Nancy. I'm coming to get you."

He hung up. Dropped the phone on the floor. Stomped it into pieces.

Nancy Corbane stared at her phone in horror. She looked around the ballroom, as if she could have had a hope of being saved had someone been there. This was Kaiser Corbane. No one could ever escape him. No one could ever survive him. No one has ever confronted him and lived to tell the tale.

She knew this was the end.

Tense, Nancy stuffed her phone into her purse. Took out a Desert Eagle. Put it to her head. "Fuck that shit."

Bang.

Works by Alexander Engel-Hodgkinson

Clockworld (One-Shot)

The Tea Party Affair

I Keep My True Love in the Basement (One-Shot)

Reality Glitch ('Jumping for Charlotte' segment)

No Bounds ('Cranston & Layman' segment)

I Keep My True Love in the Basement/REMIX

Cobalt Christmas

She Watches Me Bury Her

The Final Apocalypse Saga (First two volumes previously published as 'Dark-Boy')

Cobalt Rogue, Vol. 1: The Dead Blue

Cobalt Rogue, Vol. 2: Sky Japan Welcome Party

www.ingramcontent.com/pod-product-compliance
Lightning Source LLC
Chambersburg PA
CBHW030548130626
46552CB00006B/2485